PRAISE FOR ÖDÖN VON HORVÁTH

"Horváth had turned his back on the mournful realism of the émigrés, with their passion for easy caricature and their desire for revenge. He had realized with extraordinary acuteness that to meet the horror of reality with a horror literature was no longer possible or useful; that the reality of Fascism was in fact so overwhelming and catastrophic that no realism, particularly the agonized naturalism of the twentieth century, could do it justice."

—ALFRED KAZIN

"Ödön von Horváth was a brilliant German writer.... He makes the truth irresistible." —EDMUND WILSON

"The most gifted writer of his generation." —STEFAN ZWEIG

"Horváth is better than Brecht." —PETER HANDKE

"One of the best Austrian writers ... In every line of his prose there is an unmistakable hatred for the kind of German philistinism that made the German murder, the Third Reich, possible."

—JOSEPH ROTH

YOUTH WITHOUT GOD

ÖDÖN VON HORVÁTH (1901–1939) was born near Trieste, the son of a Hungarian diplomat who moved the family constantly. Horváth would subsequently say of himself, "I am a mélange of Old Austria; Hungarian, Croat, Czech, German; alas, nothing Semitic." Although his first language was Hungarian, he went to high school in Vienna and college in Munich, and began writing plays in German. Leaving school, he settled in Berlin, where in 1931 his play *Italian Night* debuted to rave reviews—except from the Nazi press, which reviled him. His next play, *Tales from the Vienna Woods*, starring Peter Lorre, drew an even stronger, equally divided response. When the Nazis came to power in 1933 Horváth relocated to Vienna, but on the day of the Anschluss—March 13, 1938—he fled to Budapest, and soon after, to Paris. On June 1, 1938, Horváth was caught in a storm after leaving a theater on the Champs-Élysées. He took shelter under a tree that was struck by lightning; a falling limb killed him instantly. He was 36 years old and had published 21 plays and three novels—*A Child of Our Time*, *The Eternal Philistine*, and *Youth Without God*.

LIESL SCHILLINGER is a critic and translator whose work has appeared in *The New York Times*, *The New Yorker*, *The New Republic*, and *The Washington Post*. She is the translator of *Every Day, Every Hour* by Nataša Dragnić and the forthcoming *Camille* by Alexandre Dumas.

R. WILLS THOMAS'S (1908–1955) translations from French and German include Ödön von Horváth's *A Child of Our Time*.

THE NEVERSINK LIBRARY

*I was by no means the only reader of books on board the
Neversink. Several other sailors were diligent readers,
though their studies did not lie in the way of belles-lettres.
Their favourite authors were such as you may find at the
book-stalls around Fulton Market; they were slightly physi-
ological in their nature. My book experiences on board of
the frigate proved an example of a fact which every book-
lover must have experienced before me, namely, that though
public libraries have an imposing air, and doubtless contain invaluable volumes, yet, somehow, the books that prove
most agreeable, grateful, and companionable, are those we
pick up by chance here and there; those which seem put into
our hands by Providence; those which pretend to little, but
abound in much.* —HERMAN MELVILLE, *WHITE JACKET*

YOUTH WITHOUT GOD

ÖDÖN VON HORVÁTH

TRANSLATED BY R. WILLS THOMAS

INTRODUCTION BY LIESL SCHILLINGER

MELVILLE HOUSE PUBLISHING
BROOKLYN · LONDON

YOUTH WITHOUT GOD

Originally published in German as *Jugend ohne Gott*
by Ödön von Horváth

Originally published in the United States by The Dial Press
under the title *The Age of the Fish* in 1939

This edition © Melville House 2012

Translated by R. Wills Thomas

Introduction © Liesl Schillinger

Design by Christopher King

First Melville House printing: August 2012

Melville House Publishing
145 Plymouth Street
Brooklyn, NY 11201

www.mhpbooks.com

ISBN: 978-1-61219-119-5

Printed in the United States of America
1 2 3 4 5 6 7 8 9 10

Library of Congress Control Number: 2012936545

CONTENTS

INTRODUCTION:
NO GOD BUT MEN

BY LIESL SCHILLINGER

Ödön von Horváth's Youth Without God, *and the devilry of ungodly times*

What does it mean, and why does it matter, to find yourself in godless times—particularly if you yourself are not what you would call "religious," at least, not in fair weather?

In 1933 in Vienna, five years before Germany annexed Austria into the Third Reich, a Viennese author, critic, actor, and boulevardier named Egon Friedell (born Friedmann, in 1878, when Vienna was capital of the Austro-Hungarian Empire) denounced the Nazi regime as: "the Reich of the Antichrist," and wrote vehemently, "Every trace of nobility, piety, education, reason is persecuted in the most hateful and base manner by a rabble of depraved bootblacks." Three days into the Anschluss, on March 16, 1938, Friedell jumped to his death from the window of his townhouse on the Gentzgasse when the SA came knocking. Three days before, Friedell's good friend Ödön von Horváth, the prolific playwright and novelist (born in 1901 in the Austro-Hungarian port city of Fiume, which today is called Rijeka, and lies in Croatia), had prudently packed his belongings and left Vienna, ending up in Paris after a brief sojourn in Budapest. For decades, Vienna had been an enlightened, secular haven for culture and café society. No longer.

Von Horváth, unlike Friedell, was not Jewish; nor was he much of a churchgoer. He was a sophisticated Hungarian—a diplomat's son—and had been schooled in Budapest, Vienna and Munich before moving to Berlin in his twenties to participate in the theater scene. His writing was irreverent, original and hostile to euphemism, and his two-dozen-odd plays and handful of novels mirrored his thoughts on the social, sexual and political hypocrisies of his era—a dangerous transparency in the anti-intellectual times that accompanied Hitler's rise. His 1931 comic drama *Italian Night*, in which two different parties are accidentally booked in a Bavarian pub on the same date—one a crowd of vociferous Fascists marking "German Day," the other a group of left-wingers celebrating "Italian Night"— infuriated German authorities. Light-hearted as the play's jabs may have seemed to Berlin theatergoers who didn't pick up on its subtext, von Horváth's rubber bullets made him vulnerable to return fire of a more serious kind. In 1933, after Hitler became Chancellor, the playwright's work was banned in Germany, and he fled for safety to Vienna. There in 1938, as a man of wit and conscience and something of a visionary as well, he could not help but perceive the existential threat that brown-shirted thugs posed to Viennese café society. A man does not need to be a fervent believer to sense the absence of God, or to detect the presence of darker agency.

The year before he left Vienna, von Horváth wrote the novel *Youth Without God*, which you now hold in your hands. It was published in Amsterdam in 1937, and in 1939, came out in English. Rich in parable, urgent in tone, and unusually earnest for the sly and mischievous von Horváth, the book takes the form of the diary of an unnamed teacher at a boys' school, who gets in trouble when he refuses to endorse the Aryan worldview. One of his students, "N" (the teacher identifies his pupils by initial letter only) turns in an essay in which he has written that: "All niggers are dirty, cunning, and contemptible." [p. 6] Although this sort of racial propaganda was ubiquitous during the corrupting epoch in which the book is set (the teacher recalls having heard similar slurs broadcast from loudspeakers in public places) he refuses to let it pass unreproved. "You shouldn't have said that it doesn't matter whether the negroes live or die," he scolds the boy, as he hands back the essay. "They're human too, you know." [10]

This (apparently) inflammatory comment is promptly reported by N. to his father, a local baker, who storms into the school and accuses the teacher of having made "an outrageous remark" [11] by voicing the "odious sentiment" that "negroes" are human. "It's sabotage—sabotage of the Fatherland!" the father roars. The teacher has "spread the poisonous slime of your humanitarianism" to the students, he charges. N's father takes the case to the school's headmaster; a confrontation that both he and the teacher deem their "Philippi"—referring to the historic battle (42 B.C.) in which the armies of Mark Antony and Octavian avenged Caesar's death by defeating the armies of his assassins, Brutus and Cassius. In the same spirit, the baker means to avenge the teacher's supposed slight against the Führer; while the teacher tacitly accepts the role of Brutus. The headmaster averts conflict by letting the teacher off with a warning to be sensible and keep in mind "the times we live in." [14] It's startling to realize how accurately, in 1937, von Horváth anticipated the extent of the moral rot that National Socialist ideology would foment in the young. His narrator senses that the only defense against the pervasive psychic poison is flight. The individual must act to protect and serve his own conscience, at whatever cost. Unfortunately, an entire population cannot flee en masse; and most people won't make the attempt, however toxic their environment. The narrator does not say so; but the author knows this to be true; and the weight of this knowledge gives this deceptively ingenuous fable its surprising gravitas.

As he develops his story, von Horváth follows the teacher and his class on a junior ROTC-style camping expedition, during which adults and children lose their compasses, both morally and literally, as violent and dishonorable deeds take place, testing the proposition that anyone can lead by example during a lawless era—imagine *Lord of the Flies*, with no lord, and with the addition of grown-ups who are just as selfish and wilful as Golding's marooned children. "Everything is permissible?" the teacher marvels incredulously, shocked by the unsoundness of the Nazi philosophy. "Murder, robbery, arson, perjury—these are not only allowed, there simply can be no wrong in them if they are in the interest of the cause." [19] As he rues the sclerosis of his pupils' humanity, he wonders, "What sort of a generation will theirs be? Hard? Or only brutal?" By now, everyone knows the answer to that question. Two millennia before, the Roman orator Cicero had deplored the character of his own countrymen, crying: "O tempora! O mores!" . . . and it bears remembering that he was beheaded for disloyalty to Caesar the year before Philippi; when there was as yet no Paris to offer him sanctuary. The crimes that unfold during the school camping expedition bring on a trial; but the question von Horváth implicitly poses, is this one: in an age of misrule, who is competent to stand in judgment?

In nearly all of his other writing, von Horváth exhilarates readers with cold-splash satire, lip-smacking seediness (bathroom scenes, STDs, spying, lying, petty thievery, slovenliness), un-airbrushed portrayals of ordinary *Volk*, and brashly confident political observation. His slim but potent dagger of a novel, *The Eternal Philistine*, (1930) mocked the amorality of the late 1920s by sending up the shady dealings of a pair of skirt-chasing, money-grubbing cheats (a businessman and a journalist) who head to Barcelona World's Fair, in search of easy women and easy living. But *Youth Without God* shows little of the irony that characterizes von Horváth's usual style. The barbs in this book aren't zingers or razor etchings of sordid characters, they pop out like snags of despair, catching and tearing at the European social fabric. The teacher in *Youth Without God* grieves at the obduracy of the boys in his charge. "Thinking is a process they hate," he reflects. "They turn up their noses at human beings. They want to be machines—screws, knobs, belts, wheels—or better still, munitions—bombs, shells, shrapnel." [18] His revulsion at his pupils,' colleagues' and fellow citizens' prevailing mindset is palpable; so is his sadness, and his sense of powerlessness. The conclusion one draws, reading this allegorical, prophetic work, is that in 1937, as the Anschluss approached, von Horváth correctly understood the virulence of the degradation, militarization and cruelty that were overtaking the countries around him and infecting the minds of young people, and could not laugh at it.

In France, in the spring of 1938, the author, by some reports, was meeting with a filmmaker to discuss adapting *Youth Without God* for the movies. But on June 1, only a few months after he had left Vienna, he was killed. He did not die of an act of aggression by the Reich's enforcers, he died in a freak accident on the boulevards of Paris, across from the Théâtre Marigny. A thunderstorm broke a limb off a tree, which fell on von Horváth, killing him. Had he survived that spate of Parisian bad weather, and had the Third Reich come to a less protracted and horrific end, it's tempting to ask if he might have altered the screenplay of his novel; if he might have made it less raw, less portentous, more satirical, more in the mood of his other work. In the event, though, he did not survive; and the corrosion of national character he foresaw in his novel, warning against the advent of days when "the souls of men, my friend, will become as rigid as the face of a fish" was worse than any seer could have predicted.

One of the most moving passages in all of literature appears in the *Aeneid*, which Virgil wrote in the decades immediately after the Battle of Philippi—that contest that serves as such a crucial touchpoint in *Youth Without God*. Reading von Horváth's book summons recollections of Virgil's account of the horrific end of Priam, that venerable, once mighty king of Troy. Priam has seen his city invaded, his people ravaged, and his court overrun by a brutal army. In his last minutes of life, frail but still courageous, he buckles on a younger man's suit of armor and rushes at the massed foe. But in front of his eyes, the pitiless soldier Pyrrhus stabs Priam's young son Polites to death. In grief and outrage, the king cries out (in the Robert Fitzgerald translation):

"'For what you've done, for what you've dared,' he said, 'If there is care in heaven for atrocity, May the gods render fitting thanks, reward you / As you deserve. You forced me to look on / At the destruction of my son: defiled / A father's eyes with death.'"

After Priam throws his spear at the warrior and misses, Pyrrhus drags him by the hair to an altar to Zeus, where he plunges his sword into his body, up to the hilt. What will become of the dead king? Will Priam posthumously receive the honors due him? No. "On the distant shore / The vast trunk headless lies without a name."

The force of these lines comes from their two-part encapsulation of the worst-case-scenario of the before-and-after consequences of living in a godless age. No divine justice will come: not before death, and not after it; not for the old, and not for the young. This was the worst-case-scenario that Europe faced in 1937, when *Youth Without God* was composed.

Anyone who opens this book expecting to find von Horváth's customary jaded breeziness will be struck rather by abundant Classical and religious allusions: to Philippi (of course); to the Roman Empire; to Julius Caesar; [56] and to Jesus Christ [54–5 passim] himself. Brooding on the fall of the Roman Empire, thinking of his own present-day, von Horváth's teacher envisions: "new hordes, new peoples. Arming, arming, waiting." [55] Despite the simplicity of his journal entries, the homiletic quality of his conversations and the chalky breath of the schoolroom; and notwithstanding the Boy's Own set dressing of camp and tents and sleeping bags; the teacher's diary quite intentionally, and presciently, exudes the aura of Classical tragedy.

The same preoccupation that haunts the players in the *Aeneid*—the realization that the Greco-Roman gods, during the prolonged moment of Virgil's tale, not only have no care for atrocity, but often *fuel* it (particularly spiteful Juno), haunts von Horváth's teacher in the Christian era. If Virgil's predecessor Homer can be believed, men of earlier times had confidence that the gods took an interest in their fortunes. Virgil's gods showed less benevolence. Aeneas and his entourage, vanquished and adrift, could not benefit from the consolation that fortified Odysseus, because the gods were not on their side and were not just; they were capricious, even malicious. The misery of the refugees on their hard-won road to Rome—their excruciating losses, arduous travels, and heaped misfortunes— is compounded by their sense of abandonment. Erratic behavior on Olympus had queered their fates and confounded the rules by which they lived; making their survival precarious, and their suffering meaningless—salved only by the far-off promise of the new city they will eventually establish. This was precisely the plight in which Ödön von Horváth found himself and his continent in 1937; and the plight that motivates the book he wrote in his last year of life. Divinity had fled; and no Rome beckoned on the horizon as excuse or incentive.

Two thousand years after the demise of Virgil and the Greco-Roman pantheon, and more than a century after Nietzsche declared in *The Gay Science* that "God is dead," and that, moreover, "we have killed him;" the mystery of the role that God plays—or does not play—in human affairs continues to compel authors, theologians, readers, and indeed, most thinking people. It's safe to say that the rumor of God's death that Nietzsche started 130 years ago has been exaggerated. And yet, in the 21ˢᵗ century, the questions that the philosopher raised on the heels of his inflammatory proclamation remain unanswered: "How shall we comfort ourselves, the murderers of all murderers?" and "What water is there for us to clean ourselves? What festivals of atonement, what sacred games shall we have to invent?"

These questions of solace, guilt and atonement stung even more sharply in the last century during Hitler's murderous dictatorship, which acquired its full strength after von Horváth was dead, and expired, ignominiously, less than a decade afterwards. If God exists, the atheist taunts, and the boulevardier asks with regretful politesse: how could he permit infernal states like the Third Reich to arise? In *Youth Without God*, von Horváth puts one possible answer in the words of a disgraced priest, [47] who explains to the demoralized narrator that the state "is a necessity of nature, and it is willed by God." But what if the state is a bad state; what if its structure collapses? the teacher presses. "Very often such a collapse is the will of God," the priest responds. He adds, "God is the most terrible thing in the world." [50]

In *Youth Without God*, with unique sincerity and unique power, von Horváth suggests that men who play God are more terrible still.

YOUTH WITHOUT GOD

1. NIGGERS

25th March.

THERE WERE FLOWERS ON MY TABLE. BEAUTIFUL.
A present from my landlady, kindly old soul: a birthday
present.

But I needed to use the table, and I pushed the flowers
aside, together with the letter from my people. "For your
thirty-fourth birthday," my mother wrote, "I send you the
very best wishes, my dear child. May Almighty God bring
you health, luck, and happiness." And my father: "For your
thirty-fourth birthday, my dear boy, I wish you the very
best. Almighty God give you luck, health, and happiness."

Well, luck will always come in useful, I thought—and
thank your stars you've got your health into the bargain.
Touch wood. But happiness? No, happiness I've missed. No
one, really, is happy.

I sat down at my table and uncorked my bottle of red
ink: it got onto my fingers and I was annoyed. Somebody
ought to invent an ink which would put an end to stained
fingers ...

No, I can't call myself a happy man.

Don't be so silly, I said to myself. You've got a safe job

13

with a pension at the end of it. Isn't that something in these days, when nobody knows what to-morrow holds? How many fellows would almost give an arm to be in your shoes? For what a tiny percentage of candidates for the teaching profession succeed in getting good posts in the end! Be thankful that your post is in a county high school, where you can grow old and senile without a moment of real worry. Why, you might live to be a hundred—the oldest inhabitant of the Fatherland! Then, on your birthday, you'd have your photo in the illustrated newspapers. "He is still in possession of all his faculties," you would read beneath it. That's where the pension would come in! Think it over, and count your blessings.

I did: and I began working.

Twenty-six blue copy-books lay before me—I've twenty-six boys in my charge, fourteen-year-olds; for yesterday's geography lesson they wrote me an essay. Geography and history are my subjects.

Outside, the sun was brilliant. It must have been fine in the park! Well, work's work. Must get on correcting the essays and put down the marks in my register even though I know how meaningless these marks are.

The subject set for the essay was this: "Why do we need colonies?" . . . Yes, why do we need colonies? Let's hear what they've got to say.

The first pupil whose book I opened had a name beginning with B. Bauer. Franz Bauer. There are no A's in my class, but to balance that there are five B's. Curious, that—so many B's in a class of only twenty-six. But two of them are twins. Automatically I ran down the list of names in my register, to discover again that the B's are no distance from the S's. There are four S's, three M's, two each beginning with E, G, L, and R, but only one to represent F, H, N, T, W, and Z. Names beginning with A, C, D, I, O, P, Q, U, V, X, Y do not figure on my list.

Now, Franz Bauer, why do we need colonies?

"We need colonies," he had written, "because we need numerous raw materials; without raw materials we cannot keep our home industries working at high pressure. This would have disastrous consequences: our workmen, here at home, would once more be without work." Quite true, my dear Bauer. "The workers are not the only party concerned: the whole of the nation is involved. The workers are ultimately a part of that whole."

Well, ultimately, that's a great discovery, isn't it, I thought. And it occurred to me at that moment how often to-day the most ancient platitudes are disguised as up-to-the-minute slogans! Or have they always been?

I don't know.

But I knew I'd got to get on with my task of correcting twenty-six essays—essays packed with false theories and distorted conclusions. Wouldn't it be nice for us if the very meaning of words like "false" and "distorted" were unknown to us—but there, they are only too familiar, and they go strolling arm in arm and singing their vain lays.

I must be careful: I'm a State employé. It wouldn't do for me to venture the tiniest criticism. Even if silence irks me— what good could one man do? He must keep his anger to himself. I mustn't lose my temper.

Get on with your correcting. You want to go to the cinema to-night.

Well, what's this that N's written? I found myself

reading: "All niggers are dirty, cunning, and contemptible." What rubbish! Cross it out.

I was on the point of writing in the margin, "An unsound generalization," when I pulled myself up. Hadn't I recently heard this very opinion of niggers? Where was it? Yes—it came out of the loud-speaker in a restaurant where I was having dinner—and quite took my appetite away.

So I let N's sentence stand. For it is not for a schoolmaster to question the opinions stated on the radio.

And while I read on, there was the radio still droning and cackling and vibrating through my mind: the newspapers re-echoed it and the children wrote it down like a dictation.

Soon I'd got as far as T: beneath his book lay Z's. Where was W? Had I mislaid his work? No, he was poorly yesterday—caught a bad cold at the Stadium on Sunday—inflammation of the lungs. I remember now, his father wrote me a note. All in order. Poor W! What were you doing at the Stadium, with that icy rain storming down?

Well, you might as well ask yourself what you were doing there! You were at the Stadium too on Sunday, you stuck it out till the whistle went, although neither of the teams was at all in the first class. Why?—play was slow, tedious even—why did you stay? You, along with thirty thousand other spectators?

Why?

When the outside right outplays the left half and centres, when the centre-forward breaks away and shoots, when the goalkeeper throws himself on the ball, when the back's attempt to clear brings a free kick and a spectacular save, whether the play's fair or foul, the referee good or weak-willed, impartial or the reverse—then for all those onlookers nothing exists in the world outside the game. The sun may shine or it may be pouring or snowing. It makes no difference to them. They've forgotten everything.

What is "everything" for them?...

I had to smile: the niggers, perhaps—

2. RAIN

NEXT MORNING, AS I WENT INTO THE HIGH school, on going upstairs to the masters' common-room I heard quite an uproar coming from above me. I raced up and saw five of my youngsters—E, G, R, H, and T—laying into one opponent, F.

"What's going on here?" I shouted. "If you really want to brawl like board-school boys, then have it out one with another and not five against one—that's a rotten thing to do."

They all looked up dumbly at me—even F, the victim of the attack. His collar was torn.

"What's he done to you?" I inquired; my heroes weren't very ready with an explanation. Nor was the bullied one. At last, I learned that F had done nothing to the other five. Quite the reverse—they had taken his bread roll—not to eat it themselves, but just to see him without one. They'd thrown it through the window into the yard.

I looked down. There it lay, bright on the dark asphalt in the falling rain.

Perhaps the other five had no rolls, I thought, and they were mad when they saw F's. But no, they all had them. G had two. Once more I asked:

"Why did you do it?"

They didn't know themselves. There they stood, in front

of me, grinning awkwardly. Man must be evil: so we read in the Bible. When the rain ceased, and the waters of the flood began to recede, God said: "I will not again curse the ground any more for man's sake; for the imagination of man's heart is evil from his youth."

Has God kept His promise? I cannot tell.

But I did not ask them again why they threw the bread out into the yard. I only asked them if they had never heard of that unwritten law, which for measureless thousands of years has grown stronger and stronger, to become a beautiful human precept: "If you must fight, then fight one against one. Be just." I turned to the five again.

"Aren't you rather ashamed of yourselves?" I asked.

They weren't. I seemed to be talking another language to them. They stared at me, and even the victim, F, smiled. There was derision in his smile.

"Shut the window," I said. "Or the rain will come in."

They obeyed me.

What sort of a generation will theirs be?

Hard? Or only brutal?

I said no more, and went on to the common-room. On the stairs I stopped. Had they begun again? No, all was quiet. Perhaps they were pondering my words.

3. THE RICH PLEBEIANS

FROM TEN O'CLOCK TILL ELEVEN WAS ONE OF my geography periods. I must give out the essays on the colonial question which I had marked the day before. I have mentioned already that in accordance with instructions one could say little against the contents of these compositions.

So while distributing them, I confined my observations to a few remarks on style, spelling, and sentence formation. For instance, I told B—one of the B's—that he mustn't keep going over the left margin. R should have spaced his work better. Z should know that the plural of colony isn't spelt with a "y." Only when I came to N, I couldn't pass it over.

"You've said in your essay," I told him, "that we white peoples are far in advance of the negroes in civilization and culture, and you're quite right. But you shouldn't have said that it doesn't matter whether the negroes live or die. They're human too, you know."

He looked up at me very steadily for a moment, and a hostile expression ran like a shadow over his face. Or was I mistaken? He took his note-book, nodded very correctly, and sat down again in his place.

I was soon to discover that I had not been mistaken.

For only next day, N's father showed up during my "parents' hour"—the hour I set aside once a week to keep in touch with my boys' people. They come to me to inquire about their children's progress and ask a lot of questions, most of which are very unimportant. Tradesmen, officials, officers, business men—such are my boys' fathers. Not a working-class man among them.

With many of them, I have the impression that the thoughts which their sons' essays inspire in them are very similar to mine. But we just meet and smile and talk about the weather. Most of these fathers are older than I. One of them is hoary with age! The youngest was only twenty-eight two weeks ago. He married at seventeen—a manufacturer's daughter. He's a very smart fellow. When he turns up, it is always in his open sports car. His wife stays in the car and I can see her from up here. At least, I can see her hat, her arms, and her legs.

You could have a son too, I have thought to myself: but I can easily control any wish I have to bring a son into the world. To be shot down in some war . . .

N's father confronted me. He had a very self-assured manner and looked squarely into my eyes.

"I'm Otto N's father," he began.

"I'm delighted to meet you, Mr. N," I responded with a bow; of course, I invited him to sit down, but he would not.

"My presence here," he went on, "is due to a somewhat serious occurrence. An occurrence which might well have grave consequences. My son Otto told me yesterday afternoon—and he was highly indignant about it—that you, his teacher, had made an outrageous remark—"

"I?"

"You, sir!"

"When?"

"During your geography lesson yesterday. Your pupils wrote an essay on the colonial question, and you remarked to my Otto: 'Negroes are human too.' You understand me?"

"No."

I was speaking the truth: I didn't. He looked at me, summing me up. God, what a stupid fool he looked.

"My presence here," he continued, pompously emphatic, "arises from the fact that from my earliest years I have struggled for what is just. And now I put you this question—did you voice that odious sentiment of yours on the negro question, in that class and at that time—or did you not?"

"I did," I answered with a smile I could not restrain. "Your presence here, otherwise—"

"Please," he interrupted me sharply. "I am not in a mood for joking. You don't know yet what the expression of such a sentiment about negroes implies. It's sabotage—sabotage of the Fatherland! Oh, don't pretend you are not aware of it! I know only too well the secret ways in which you try to undermine the souls of these innocent children, and how you spread the poisonous slime of your humanitarianism among them."

This was a bit too much.

"Forgive me," I broke in, "you can find that in the Bible—that all of us, all men, are human."

"When the Bible was written, there were no colonies as we understand them," continued N's baker-father, impervious as a block of stone. "You can't take the Bible in an exact sense—you've got to take it figuratively, or not at all. Do you believe, sir, for instance, that Adam and Eve actually lived—or do you admit there's a mythological element in the story? You see? I'll take good care that we'll have no more expatiations on the love of God from you."

"You needn't," I muttered, showing him out. I was almost throwing him out.

"We'll meet again at Philippi!" he shouted to me as he disappeared.

Two days later, I stood at Philippi.

The Head had sent for me.

"I wanted to tell you," he began, "that yesterday I had a letter from the authorities. A baker, named N, it seems, has lodged a complaint about you. Apparently you have expressed certain opinions. Now, I'm quite *au fait*, and I know how such complaints come to be made—there's no need for you to do any explaining. But, my dear colleague, it's my duty to warn you that nothing like this must occur again. You're forgetting the private memorandum that went round—number 5679, paragraph 33! We are supposed to keep youth at a distance from everything which doesn't in some way or another train their minds for war—which means, morally, we must prepare them to be warriors. Just that."

I glanced at the Head. He was smiling. As if he guessed my thoughts. Then he rose, and walked up and down. A fine old figure.

"It may set you wondering," he said suddenly, "to hear me blowing the bugles of war! And you wouldn't be wrong. You're thinking, What sort of a fellow is this? Only a few years ago he used to subscribe to ardent peace propaganda—and to-day? To-day he's all for the slaughter."

"I'm aware that it's only because you're forced to be," I murmured, to reassure him.

He pricked up his ears, came to a stop in front of me, and searched me with keen eyes.

"Young man," he said, gravely enough, "one thing you must be sure of—there is no compulsion. I could—yes, I could—struggle against the spirit of the times, and have myself put in jail through the agency of our worthy baker.

I could resign this position, but I don't intend to—I won't. I want to reach the age-limit and draw my full pension."

Excellent, I thought.

"You'll think I'm a cynic," he continued, and his manner was now quite fatherly. "All of us, striving and aspiring towards better things for mankind, have forgotten one thing: the times we live in. My dear colleague, a man who's seen as much as I have gradually acquires a sense of reality."

It's all right for you, went my thoughts, you lived in time to see that hey-day before the war. But what about me? It was in the last year of the war that I loved for the first time—what, I am not sure.

The Head nodded sadly.

"We live in a plebeian world. Think of the Rome of old, the Rome of 287 B.C. The struggle between patricians and plebs still hadn't been settled, but the plebeians were already in possession of the highest State offices."

"Forgive me, sir," I ventured, "so far as my knowledge goes, no poor plebeians hold the reins of power with us. The great, the one and only power, is gold."

His eyes came to rest on mine again, and he smiled slyly.

"Yes, but I can't give you a satisfactory mark in history, though you may be an historian! You've forgotten that there were the rich plebeians too. Remember now?"

I remembered. Of course! The rich plebeians, who deserted the people and who, together with the already decadent patricians, built up the new nobility of office— the so-called Optimates.

"Don't forget that."

"I shan't."

4. BREAD

WHEN I AGAIN ENTERED THE CLASSROOM IN which I had permitted myself to say something in favour of the negroes, I experienced the sudden feeling that all was not well. Had these gentry smeared ink on my chair? No. Why were they looking at me like that, as if they were quietly revelling in the thought of my discomfiture?

Some one raised his hand. What did that mean? He came up to me and made a little bow as he handed me a letter. Then he went back to his place.

What was wrong?

I opened the letter, glanced over it, and though I should have liked a minute longer, I controlled my curiosity and gave the impression of having read enough. Yes, every one had signed it—the whole twenty-five. W was still poorly.

"We do not wish"—that letter read—"to be taught by you, for after what has occurred we, the undersigned, have lost our confidence in you, and would prefer another teacher."

I glanced at "the undersigned." My eyes went from one to another of them. They were silent and avoided my gaze. I counted ten, and asked as casually as I could:

"Who wrote this?"

No one came forward.

"Don't be such cowards!"

My words had no effect.

"Good," I went on, rising from my table, "it doesn't interest me at all, any more than it does you, which of you is responsible for writing this, since every one of you has signed it. And I too have not the slightest wish to go on teaching a class which has lost confidence in me. Believe me, with the best conscience in the world, I—"

I stopped, having suddenly noticed one boy writing behind his desk.

"What are you writing down there?"

He tried to keep the paper hidden.

"Bring it here."

I took it from him. He smiled scornfully. He had put down in shorthand every word I had said.

"Ah! So you want to spy on me?"

They grinned.

Grin on, I despise you! By God, I've nothing more to lose here. Let some other fellow try and grapple with you . . .

I went to the Head, told him what had happened and made my request to be given another class. He smiled.

"D'you think the others will be any better?"

He accompanied me back to my classroom. He stormed, he shouted, he raved—a magnificent piece of acting! It was an outrage, he roared, a mean, caddish trick—they had no right whatever, the louts, to ask for another teacher, had they all gone mad—and so on and so on . . . And then he left me alone with them.

There they sit facing me, full of hatred. They'd like to ruin me—to blot out my whole existence, because they can't bear to think that niggers are human too! Are they—human? No.

But wait, my friends. I'm not going to get into any trouble on your account, and I'm certainly not going to lose my job—and have nothing to eat, eh? No clothes, no shoes! No roof over my head? Wouldn't you like that! But from now on, I'll let you believe that there are no human beings besides yourselves, I'll go on drumming that into you until the niggers come and roast you! That's what you're asking for, and you shall get it.

5. PESTILENCE

THAT NIGHT I HAD NO WISH TO GO TO BED. Those shorthand notes were still in my mind's eye. Yes, they wanted to destroy mė.

If they were Indians, they'd have tied me to a post and had my scalp, without the slightest thought that they might be wrong.

They're so confident that they're doing the right thing.

They're a nasty crowd.

Or is it that I don't understand them? I'm thirty-four: am I too old for them already? Is there a deeper gulf between us than between other generations?

I think it's an unbridgeable gulf.

If these fellows merely rejected everything that's still sacred to me—well, that wouldn't be so bad. What hurts is that they put it aside without even having known it. Worse still, they haven't the slightest desire to know it.

Thinking is a process they hate.

They turn up their noses at human beings. They want to be machines—screws, knobs, belts, wheels—or better still, munitions—bombs, shells, shrapnel. How readily they'd die on a battlefield! To have their name on some war memorial—that's the dream of their puberty.

Steady, though—isn't there something admirable there—in that readiness for the supreme sacrifice?

Yes—if the cause is a just one.

But what would be their cause?

Whatever benefits our race is right, drones the radio. Whatever hinders us is wrong.

So everything is permissible? Murder, robbery, arson, perjury—these are not only allowed, there simply can be no wrong in them if they are in the interest of the cause.

The attitude of the lawless.

When the rich plebeians in old Rome feared that the people might succeed through their plan to reduce taxes, they sheltered behind a dictatorship. And they condemned to death for high treason the patrician Manlius Capitolinus, who with his riches had tried to free their plebeian debtors from their debts. They hurled him down from the Tarpeian Rock.

Since the very existence of human society, the need for self-preservation has driven men to commit crimes. But those crimes were secret deeds, men hushed them up and were ashamed of them.

But to-day men are proud of them. There is a pestilence among us.

All of us are tainted, friend and foe alike. Our souls are great black sores, and life is dying in them. They die, and we live on. And my soul too is poor and weak ... When I read in the paper that one of them has died, my mind finds words—"Too few are dead, too few."

To-day—even to-day—haven't I been thinking, "Die—all of you. Get out!"

But I don't want to keep thinking that ...

I had a wash and went out to a café I know, where you are bound to find some one to play chess with. I wanted to be free of my room, to be outside its narrow walls.

The flowers my landlady gave me for my birthday had faded. They would soon be withered.

To-morrow was Sunday.

In the café I found no one I knew. Not a soul. What should I do next? I went into the cinema. And in the news-reel I saw the rich plebeians. They were unveiling memorials to themselves, they were turning the first sods and inspecting their life-guards on parade. Then followed a cartoon, with Mickey out-witting the most formidable of cats. And then a thrilling crime picture, in which a good deal of shooting went to further the principle that good must triumph in the end.

When I came out of the cinema, it was night. But I didn't go home. My room held fears for me.

Across the road was a little bar—a minor night-club. I thought I'd step inside for a drink, if it didn't turn out to be too dear.

I found it quite cheap.

I went inside. A lady wanted to keep me company.

"You are all alone?" She smiled.

"Yes—unfortunately—"

"No."

She drew back—slunk back as if hurt. I didn't wish you any harm, really! You shouldn't have let it hurt you.

I was alone.

6. THE AGE OF THE FISH

SOME ONE OUGHT TO INVENT A WEAPON which should nullify the effectiveness of any other weapon—the opposite of a weapon, in fact. Ah, if only I were an inventor, what wouldn't I invent! What a happy place I'd make the world. So ran my thoughts as I swallowed my sixth schnapps.

But I wasn't an inventor—would this world have missed anything if I'd never seen its light? What would the sun have had to say? And I wondered who would be living in my room now.

Don't wonder such rubbish, I told myself. You're drunk, drunk. If you hadn't been born, how would you know that your room existed? Your bed might still have been a piece of wood or a tree. Shame on you, old fool, asking metaphysical questions like a schoolboy who hasn't digested his first experiences. Don't probe into hidden secrets. You're drunk. Drink down your seventh schnapps.

I drank it, and went on. Ladies and gentlemen, I'm no friend of peace. I'd like to see us all killed off. But not a simple death. An involved death. Torture ought to be introduced again, eh? The rack. Man can't confess to guilt enough, for man is vile.

With the eighth schnapps, I was nodding to the pianist in a very friendly fashion, although his music had struck

me as rather curious at the sixth. I was quite unaware that
the man standing in front of me had already spoken to me
twice. Not until his third attempt did I glance up.

I recognized him at once—our Julius Caesar.

Once a respected colleague—senior language master
in a girls' high school—a nasty scandal had lost him his
position. The party involved was a girl beneath the age of
consent. He was sent to prison. For a long time we saw
nothing of him: then I heard that he was hawking cheap
goods from door to door. He wore an enormous tie-pin—a
death's head in miniature, in which, by means of an elec-
trical device, one solitary eye glowed red whenever he
pressed a button in his pocket. Such was the humour of
this shipwrecked life.

I'm still rather hazy as to how he suddenly came to be
sitting beside me, engaged in a heated argument. I was
very drunk, you see: all I can recollect is a few disjointed
phrases.

"Everything you're telling me, dear colleague," Julius
Caesar was saying, "is a lot of infantile trash. It is high time
you fell in with a man who's got nothing left to hope for,
and who can therefore view the transition between the
generations with a perfectly open mind. Now you and I,
colleague, according to Adam Riese, form two generations,
and those scummy fellows make another. So altogether, according to Adam Riese, that's three generations. I'm sixty,
you're, say, thirty, and those creatures are about fourteen.
Now, the experiences of puberty are decisive over the entire course of a lifetime, especially for the male sex ..."

"You're boring me," I said.

"Even if I am, you'd better listen, if you want me to keep
my temper. And so—the one great problem facing my

generation in its puberty was the other sex—women—the women we didn't get. For we didn't, in those days. So our outstanding everyday experience was self-gratification, with all that it implied in those times—anxiety over the loss of one's health, et cetera—groundless fears, of course, but we didn't know that then. In other words, women formed our stumbling-block, and we slipped into the world war. But during your puberty, colleague, the war was well under way. There weren't any men, and the ladies weren't so hesitant. You didn't have to waste your time wondering, all the unsatisfied women threw themselves onto your dawning virility. For your generation, women ceased to mean anything sacred: and so they'll never mean enough to you and your like, you'll always be hankering after something cleaner, finer, more unattainable: in other words—self-gratification. In this case, we see women finding a stumbling-block in you youngsters, and slipping into masculinity."

"Colleague," I stammered, "you're an ero—an erotomaniac."

"How so?"

"Because you behold all creation from the point of view of sex. It's characteristic of your generation, especially in its old age. But don't spend your days covered up in bed. Get out, pull the curtains aside, let in the light and have a look out. Have a look out."

"And what do we see outside?"

"Nothing very fine, but still—"

"It strikes me you're a romantic in disguise—I beg of you to stop interrupting me. Sit down. We're coming now to the third generation; for them, women simply constitute a problem no longer, for there aren't any women nowadays, all we've got is a lot of monsters who study, row, and march and develop their muscles. Has it ever occurred to you that the charm of women becomes less and less and less?"

"You're biased!"

"Who could wax enthusiastic over a Venus with a ruck-sack? Not I. Ah, yes, the unhappy part of it for the youth of to-day is that they no longer have any puberty, in the right sense—an erotic, political, moral experience—they don't get it, it's all pitched overboard. And besides that, too many defects are celebrated as victories, and too often the inner-most feelings of youth are laughed at: while in other ways they're made too comfortable. They've got to take down what the radio bellows out and then they get top marks. But there are still a few here and there, thank God—"

"Who are they?"

He looked mournfully round, crouched closer to me, and very quietly went on:

"I know a woman whose son goes to the high school. His name's Robert, and he's fifteen years old. Lately he's been reading a certain book—in secret. No, it's nothing erotic. Nihilistic. The title's this—*The Worth of Human Life*—and it's strictly forbidden."

We glanced at each other as we raised our drinks.

"So you think some of them put in a bit of secret reading?"

"I'm sure of it. There's quite a little *cénâcle* gathers round at this woman's house, she's often quite beside herself. The little fellows read everything. But they only read to criticize and condemn. They live in their paradise of stupidity and scorn is their ideal. Cold times are coming, my friend—the Age of the Fish."

"The Fish?"

"I'm only an amateur in astrology, but I know the earth's moving into the zone of the Fish. The souls of men, my friend, will become as rigid as the face of a fish."

And that is all I can recollect of my long argument with Julius Caesar. I well remember that while I was talking, he would light up his death's head from time to time to irritate me. But I didn't let him, although I was fearfully drunk—

Then I woke up in a strange room. It wasn't my own bed. In the darkness. I was aware of another person's breathing. A woman, asleep. Was she blond or a brunette? Red-headed or black? I couldn't remember. I wanted to see her. Should I turn on the light?

No, I'd just go to sleep.

But I left the bed cautiously and went over to the window.

Still night. And I could see nothing. No streets, no houses. Nothing but mist. Far off there was a lamp shining and the mist lay like water under its glimmer. My window might have looked out over the sea.

I didn't wish to see more.

Or the Fish might swim up to the window and gaze in.

7. THE GOALKEEPER

WHEN I WENT BACK TO MY ROOM NEXT DAY, MY landlady was waiting for me. She was in a very excitable state.

"There's a gentleman to see you," she said. "He's been waiting twenty minutes already. I showed him into the drawing-room. Where were you—?"

"With some friends. They live a good way out and I lost the last train, so I stayed the night."

I went into the drawing-room.

My visitor stood by the piano—an unassuming little man. He was flicking over the pages of a music-album. I didn't recognize him at once. His eyes were red. Up all night, I thought. Or could he have been crying?

"I'm W's father," he said. "You must help me, sir, something awful's happened. My boy's dying."

"What!"

"He caught a terrible cold at the Stadium last week, and the doctor says only a miracle could save him now. But miracles don't happen. His mother doesn't know the worst. I couldn't find it in me to tell her. My son's only conscious from time to time, sir, then he's off again. Delirious. But when he's conscious he's always asking to see somebody—"

"Not me?"

"No, not you, sir. It's the goalkeeper he wants to see—the

man who played such a fine game last Sunday, he says. He's
my son's hero. And I thought you might know where we
could get hold of this goalie, we might ask him to come—"

"I know where he lives," I answered. "I'll see him. You
go home. I'll bring him along."

W's father left me.

I picked up my coat and went out.

The goalkeeper lived quite close. I knew the sports-
goods shop kept by his sister.

It was a Sunday and the shop was shut, but the man had
a flat above it.

I found him at breakfast, in a room glittering with
trophies. He was ready to come straight away. He left his
breakfast and ran down the stairs ahead of me. He called a
taxi. He wouldn't let me pay.

W's father met us at the door. He seemed to have grown
even smaller.

"He's not conscious," he murmured. "The doctor's there.
But come in, sir. Thank you—thank you for coming."

The room was half dark. A bed stood in the corner.
There lay W. His face was flushed deeply, and it struck me
that he was the smallest fellow in my class. His mother too
was a tiny woman.

The big goalie stood by, a little embarrassed. So here
lay one of his most ardent admirers. One of the thousands
who had cheered him, who knew the story of his life, who
asked him for autographs, who loved to take their place
waiting behind his goal, to be dispersed by the officials.
He sat down quietly near the bed and looked down at the
child.

His mother bent over him.

"Henry!" she said. "Henry! The goalie's here!"

His eyes opened and blinked at his hero.

"Fine!" He smiled.

"You wanted to see me, didn't you?" the other said. "Well, here I am."

"When are you playing England?"

"That's a secret of the gods. There's a split in the league among the powers that be. We're having trouble over the date. I think it's likelier we'll be playing Scotland."

"You'll walk over them!"

"Oho! The Scots can shoot as quick as lightning, and from any point."

"Tell me about them."

And the goalie told some of his stories. He told of famous victories and unmerited defeats, of hostile referees and corrupted linesmen. He got up, took two chairs to make a goal and showed W how he had made two successive saves. He pointed to a scar on his forehead that he'd got in a crazy game in Lisbon. He spoke of foreign lands where he had watched over his goal as closely as if the posts had been made of gold; of Africa, where the Bedouins bring their weapons into the grandstand, and of the lovely little island of Malta, where the ground is made of stone—

While the goalie was talking, little W fell asleep. With the happiest of smiles, quiet, contented . . .

The funeral took place the next Wednesday, at half-past two in the afternoon. The March sun was shining. Easter wasn't far off.

We stood there, around the open grave. The coffin was lowered.

The Head was present, with nearly all the staff. Only the physics master was missing; he's a queer fellow.

The priest read the funeral service. W's parents and

some relatives of theirs stood motionless. Opposite us, in a half circle, stood W's contemporaries—the whole class. Twenty-five.

The flowers lay near the grave. One beautiful wreath bore, on a greenish card, the words "From your Goalkeeper."

And while the priest spoke of flowers that bloom and die, my eyes fell on N.

He stood behind L, H, and F.

I watched him. No expression betrayed itself in his face. He caught my eye.

He's your bitterest enemy, I felt with a sudden conviction. To him, you're a criminal. Beware of him when he's older. Or he'll destroy everything, even to the ruins of the memory of you. He's wishing now that you lay down there; and he'd destroy your very grave, and none should know that you had lived. But don't show that you're aware of his thoughts. Keep your own ideals to yourself. Others will come after N. Other generations. Don't think, friend N, that you can outlive what I hold holy, though you may outlive me.

And even in the midst of my thoughts, I felt that some one else was watching me. T.

He was smiling—very quietly, with a supercilious scorn. Had he guessed my thoughts? Was that the reason for that strange, fixed smile?

Two bright, round eyes, watching me. Gazing at me. Unblinking.

A fish?

8. WAR

SOME THREE YEARS AGO, THE AUTHORITIES issued an order which made changes in our Easter holidays. All schools were to go to camp for some part of them. "Camp" meant a kind of premilitary service. Our scholars must spend ten days in the open air—surrounded by the "freedom of nature": they must live in tents like soldiers, under the eye of their form-masters. Sergeants from the reserve would direct the training. Marching and exercises were the order of the day, and for those above fourteen, rifle practice. The boys were naturally enthusiastic: nor were we teachers sorry, for we weren't too old to like playing Indians.

That Easter Sunday, the inhabitants of a town, a good way off, saw a huge charabanc coming their way. The driver was blowing his horn as if he were driving a fire-engine. Geese and hens fluttered out of our way, dogs howled and the excitement spread to every one.

"Here they come. The boys! The cadets!"

At eight that morning we had left the high school and now it was half-past two as we drew up at the town hall.

The mayor greeted us, the police-inspector saluted. The head master of the town's school was there, of course, and the priest very soon appeared, a little late. A friendly looking fellow with a round face.

The mayor showed me his map of the district and explained where our camp-site lay. A good hour's journey if you didn't want to race.

"The sergeant-major's there already," announced the inspector. "And two men went on ahead early in an Army lorry, to lay out the camp."

While the boys got out and gathered their belongings together, I had another look at the map. The little town lay two thousand feet above sea-level: already we were in the neighbourhood of the great mountains which rose to six thousand feet or so; and beyond them stood others, dark and cold, capped with eternal snow.

"What's this?" I asked the mayor, pointing to a group of buildings which the map showed on the western outskirts of the town.

"That's our factory," he answered. "The greatest saw-mill in the district. But unfortunately it was closed down last year. Profits too small," he added with a smile. "We've got a good many unemployed now. It's distressing."

The teacher chimed in too, and told me that the saw-mill belonged to a big combine. I could see that he hadn't much sympathy for the shareholders and directors. Nor did I feel any. The town was very poor, he went on, half the people lived by piece-work, at a terrible rate of pay. One child in three was undernourished.

"Yes," chuckled the inspector. "Here too, with the beauties of nature all around!"

Before we started off for the camp, the priest came up to me.

"You're the master in charge, I believe? Just a moment. There's a little thing I'd like to bring to your notice. About an hour and a half from your camping-ground there's a castle. The State acquired it, and there are girls quartered there, round about the same age as your boys. They're running round all day and half the night, so keep a look out"—he smiled—"and see that no complaints come to my ears."

"I'll take good care."

"You don't mind my mentioning it? When you've spent thirty-five years listening to confessions, you grow rather sceptical, and a journey of a mere hour and a half doesn't strike you in the light of a deterrent."

He laughed.

"You must come along and see me some time, I've got some new wine down."

At about three o'clock we started. First through a valley, then up a winding hill-side road, from which we looked down again into the glen. There was a smell of resin in the air as our path entered a long wood. At last the trees fell back to let in the light: before us lay our site, in a meadow. The mountains were still closer to us now.

The sergeant and his two pioneers were playing cards. When they saw us coming they got up quickly and the sergeant advanced, a very military figure. About fifty, he'd be. He wore an unobtrusive pair of glasses. A decent fellow.

Now we must get down to work. The sergeant and his two men showed the youngsters how to put up a tent. I joined in. In the centre of the camp we left an empty space, and there we put up our colours. In three hours our city was built. The two pioneers saluted and started off back to the little town.

Near the flag-pole stood a biggish chest—our fire-arms. The targets were erected: wooden soldiers in foreign uniforms.

With twilight, we lit a fire and did our cooking. It smelt good. We sang a few Army songs. The sergeant drank a schnapps, and his voice grew hoarser.

The mountain-wind stirred.

"That's coming down from the glaciers," said one of the youngsters. Some of them were coughing.

I thought of the dead W.

Yes, you were the smallest fellow in the class—and the friendliest too. I believe you'd have been the only one to write nothing in your essay against the niggers. So you had to go. Where are you now?

Has an angel come and taken you—as the angels did in the old tales?

And did he fly with you to the place where all the blessed footballers play? Where the goalkeeper's an angel too, and the referee, whistling when a player flies after the ball? For that must be off-side in heaven! Are you happy up there? Of course! Up there everybody sits in the grand-stand—in the middle of the front row—while those horrid officials who always chased you out of the goal when you wanted an autograph must stand behind the giants who stop them from seeing the game—

Night now, and off to bed.

"To-morrow we start in earnest," smiled the sergeant. He shared a tent with me. He snored.

Once or twice I flashed my torch to have a look at my watch. On the tent wall I saw a brownish-red stain. What was it?

To-morrow we start in earnest, I lay thinking. In earnest. In that chest near the flag-pole lies war.

War.

We were on the battlefield.

In my mind's eye I saw the two pioneers—the sergeant from the reserve, who was in command now—and
the wooden soldiers, who would teach us how to shoot
straight. Other figures passed before me. The Head, N and
his father the baker—the baker of Philippi. I thought of
the saw-mill that now lay idle, and the stockholders, draw-
ing larger profits, even in spite of its idleness. I thought of
the smiling inspector and the priest who liked his glass
of wine, of the negroes that might not live, of the piece-
workers who couldn't live: I thought of the powers that rule
the land, and the underfed children.

And of the Fish.

We're on the battlefield here. Then where is the front?

I heard the night-wind, and the snoring of the sergeant.

Was that—blood—that brownish-red stain?

9. VENUS ON TREK

SUNLIGHT FILLED THE CAMP. WE LEFT OUR TENTS.

We washed in the brook and made tea. After breakfast the sergeant made the boys form two lines, arranging themselves according to their height. They numbered off. He divided them into squads.

"No shooting to-day," he told us. "Just a bit of exercise."

He was a sharp disciplinarian: the two lines must be in perfect order. He had a habit of squinting one eye.

"Come up a bit here—back there, you're too far forward. You're a yard in front of the others, number three there!"

Number three was Z. How hard it is for him to keep in line, I found myself thinking. Suddenly I heard N's voice.

"Back there, idiot!" he rasped at Z.

"Now, now"—from the sergeant—"don't get rough. There's no cursing in the Army now. That's a thing of the past. Get that into your heads."

N fell silent. Blushing hotly, he threw me a furtive glance. Now he could have strangled me, for it was he who was in the wrong. I felt strangely pleased, but I restrained a smile.

"Regiment—march!" came the sergeant's command. The boys marched off. The biggest in front, the smallest at the rear. Another minute, and they were in the wood. Out of sight.

Two remained behind. One of the M's and one of the B's.

They peeled potatoes and made other preparations for the midday meal. All in quiet high spirits.

"Sir!" shouted M suddenly. "Look what's on the march over there!"

I looked. Some twenty girls were marching in military formation, weighed down with rucksacks. As they approached we could hear them singing—Army songs in a trilling soprano. B laughed aloud.

Then they became aware of our camp and halted about two hundred yards away.

Their leader addressed them and came on alone in our direction. I set out to meet her.

We introduced ourselves. She was a teacher in a large provincial town and the girls were those of her class. They were staying at the castle now—so these were the young ladies to whom the priest's warning related! As I walked back with my new companion to her regiment, the girls stared at me like so many cows. I don't think the priest need have felt any anxiety: these girls didn't look very attractive.

Besmirched with sweat and grime, they were scarcely a pretty sight.

Their mistress seemed to guess my thoughts—at least she had that womanly attribute. She attempted an explanation.

"We don't go in for frills and tinsel. And we don't spend our time theorizing. We like to get something done."

I didn't want to embark on a long argument over the various schools of thought where education was concerned.

I just murmured "Ah!" as an answer, and thought to myself, Even N's a human being by the side of these poor creatures.

"Yes, we're Amazons," continued the teacher.

But the Amazons were only a myth. This was reality. Daughters of Eve, strayed far.

I thought of Julius Caesar.

He couldn't find any inspiration in Venus with a rucksack. Nor I.

Before they marched off again the teacher explained to me that to-day the girls had been out looking for the lost airman. How so?—had some 'plane crashed?

No! The search for the lost airman was a new military exercise for the nation's young womanhood. Somewhere in the wood was a big white box. The girls spread out and advanced in a wide line, each of them searching for the white box.

"It's in case of war. So that we can immediately get going if there's an actual crash. Behind the lines, of course: unfortunately women won't be at the front."

A pity!

They marched on. I watched them. A good many marches had made their short legs even shorter—and thicker.

March on, mothers of the future.

10. WEEDS

PALE SKY AND RAIN-WASHED EARTH: THE WORLD
a water-colour—"April."

I made my way back to the camp, following a footpath
across the fields. What lay behind the hill?

My path skirted a thicket in a wide curve. The air was
still, with something of the eternal stillness. No murmur,
no stir of life. The very beetles were nearly all asleep.

On the other side of the hill a farm-house stood in a
little valley. There was no one to be seen, no sign of the dog.

I was on the point of going down to it when, involuntarily, I stopped. A narrow lane led past the farm: suddenly
I had caught sight of three figures crouching behind the
hedge. Children, hiding there, two boys and a girl. The boys
would be about thirteen, the girl a year or two older. All
were barefooted. What were they doing, hiding? I waited.
One of the boys got up and started towards the farm. All at
once he stopped short and slunk back to the hedge. I heard
the creaking of a wagon. A load of timber drawn by heavy
horses went slowly by.

When it was out of sight the boy made for the farm
again, reached the door and knocked. He must have
knocked with a hammer, or so it seemed to me, the sound
rang out so sharply. Then he—and the two others—waited,
listening. The girl was standing up, peering over the hedge.

How tall she was, and thin! The door opened, and an old peasant woman appeared, bent over a stick. She looked about as if sniffing the air. The boy stood there quietly. Suddenly the old woman cried:

"Who is it?"

Why was she shouting?—there was the boy, in front of her! She shouted again:

"Who is it?" and groped with her stick, as if she could not see him. Could she be blind?

The girl pointed to the open door, as if giving an order, and on tiptoe the boy slipped into the house.

The old woman stood listening.

Yes, she was blind.

From the house came a noise—the clatter of broken crockery. The blind woman gave a frightened start and cried:

"Help! Help!"

But the girl threw herself upon her and put her hand over her mouth.

The boy came out carrying a loaf of bread and a jug, as the girl knocked the stick out of the old woman's hand. I rushed towards them. The blind woman staggered, stumbled, and fell. The three children vanished.

I helped the frightened, whimpering old woman to her feet. A peasant had heard the noise and ran up. Between us, we got her into the house, and I told him what had happened. He showed no surprise.

"Yes, they got the old lady out so as they could slip in the door. That lot again! There's no catching 'em. They're worse than magpies—a regular gang of thieves!"

"Children?"

The peasant nodded.

"Yes, they've even been at it up there at the castle, where the young ladies are. They had half their wash not so long ago. You'd better look out, or they'll be up to the same tricks in your camp."

"We'll be on the watch for them!"

"There's nothing I'd put past 'em. They're weed, and ought to be rooted up!"

11. THE LOST AIRMAN

I TURNED BACK TO THE CAMP. WE HAD REASSURED and consoled the old blind woman. She was grateful to me—why should she be? Wasn't it a matter of course?— I couldn't leave her lying there on the ground. A lot of brutes, these children.

I came to a sudden stop, for a strange mood came over me. I didn't feel at all furious over the theft of the bread, or even over the brutality that went with it—I merely condemned it. Why wasn't I outraged? Because they were poor children with nothing to eat? No, not because of that.

My path went round a great curve: I tried a short cut— quite confidently, for I have a good sense of direction. I pushed on through brambles. Here were weeds—thriving. I kept thinking of the girl—I could still see her stretching up to peep over the hedge. Was she the robber chief? I'd like to have seen her eyes—for I'm no saint.

The trees grew sparser here. What was that, a little farther on?

A white box: and marked on it, in big red letters, "AEROPLANE." The lost airman: of course! They hadn't found him yet, then.

So it was here you crashed! An aerial combat, or an anti-aircraft gun? A bomber—shattered to the ground, a black, flame-charred mass. A box.

Perhaps you weren't killed—but they couldn't find your lacerated body. Friend or foe—which were you, lost flyer? Now lost in death.

A box. A piece of cardboard.

As I stood gazing at it I heard some one speak. A woman's voice. A sad plea of a voice.

"No one can alter it."

Gently, I pushed the leafy branches aside—to see two girls from the castle. Two of those girls with the short thick legs. One was crying: a comb hung from her companion's hand.

"What do I care about the lost airman?" she sobbed. "I don't want to keep running through the wood. Look how—how swollen my legs are. I can't do any more marching. Let him die, that lost airman. I want to live. I'll run away, Anne, I'll run away. I won't sleep in the castle again, it's like a prison. I want to do my hair and wash and tidy up."

Anne tried to console her, gathering her fine hair back out of her tear-stained eyes.

"What can we girls do about it? Even the teacher's been crying lately—in secret. Mummy's always saying that men have gone mad. They make the laws."

Men?

Anne kissed her friend's forehead. I felt ashamed for having scorned that little regiment so hastily.

Perhaps Anne's mother was right. Perhaps men are mad now—those who aren't mad haven't the courage to put their maniacal fellows into strait-jackets.

They're cowards—like myself.

12. GO HOME

I REACHED THE CAMP. THE POTATOES WERE peeled and in the pot, the soup was ready steaming. The regiment was back. The boys were in high spirits, though the sergeant complained of a headache. He'd rather overdone it, but he wasn't the one to give in.

"How old d'you think I am, sir?" he asked me.

"Round the fifty mark."

"I'm sixty-three," he smiled, flattered. "Why! I was one of the last reserve way back in the war!"

I was afraid he was going to embark on a long recital of his experiences, but I needn't have been.

"We'll keep the war out of it," he muttered. "I've got three grown-up sons."

His eyes were far away as he spoke—they gazed at the mountain horizon. He took an aspirin for his headache.

A decent fellow, the sergeant.

I told him about the robber band. He sprang up, called the boys together and gave them instructions. A guard must be kept at night, four boys, changed every two hours. On all sides. The camp must be defended to the last man!

"Hurrah!" cried the youngsters, fired with enthusiasm.

"Funny," muttered the sergeant. "Headache's gone."

After our midday meal, I went down to the little town

again. I had to see the mayor on a few small matters—and we had to settle the question of supplies, for a regiment can't train on an empty stomach.

With the mayor, I found the priest. He insisted on my going along with him for a glass of wine. A congenial soul, the priest; and I'm fond of a glass.

The peasants greeted him as we walked to the rectory. He was taking the shortest way, and it led through one of the meaner streets. There were no peasants here.

"This is where the piece-workers live," I learned.

The priest perhaps glanced up at the sky.

The grey houses were wedged in rows. Children painting dolls sat in the open windows—children with old, blanched faces, and darkness behind them.

"They have to save on light," said the priest.

Then:

"I get no greeting here. They've no love for me!"

He doubled his pace, and I mine.

The children were staring strangely at me. I thought of Julius Caesar and the face of the Fish. But this was different. There was no scorn on these faces, only hate. And behind that hate, the dreary darkness reigned. They had no light. They were saving light.

The rectory was next to the church—a very substantial church. Around it lay the cemetery. Around the rectory a garden. Bells clanged in the church tower. Blue smoke trailed upwards from the rectory chimneys.

In that garden of death the white stones rose like petals. In the rectory garden, cabbages and vegetables. Tombstones there: little stone dwarfs here where we walked, and a reclining fawn, and a stone mushroom.

Everything was neat and tidy in the rectory. Not a

particle of dust in the air. While in the cemetery, nothing but dust.

The priest showed me into his charming study.

"Sit down. I'll get the wine."

He left me while he made his way to the cellar.

A picture on the wall attracted my notice. I had seen it before. My parents have a copy of it—my parents are very pious. It was not until the war that I abandoned God. It was asking too much of a youngster to understand that God could allow a war like that. I looked at the picture. God hung nailed to a cross, dead. Mary cried, and John was comforting her. Lightning played across the dark sky. In the foreground stood a warrior in helmet and armour—the Roman Captain.

I felt a longing for my home as I saw this.

I wished I were a boy again. I remember how I used to gaze out of the window in a storm—watching the low, rain-piled clouds, the lightning and the hailstones.

I thought of my first love-affair. I shouldn't want to see her now.

Go home!

I saw another scene: myself, sitting on a seat, and wondering which I would be, a teacher or a doctor?

I'm glad I became a teacher. Rather than heal the sick, I wanted to impart something to the living and the healthy. I wanted to help lay the foundation stone of a happier and lovelier age.

Go home!

Home, where you were born. What are you searching for outside the boundaries of home? I'm a teacher now—it means no delight to me. Go home!

13. HUMAN IDEALS

THE SUN ITSELF TINGLED IN THE PRIEST'S WINE. But his cakes tasted of incense. We were sitting in a corner of his study. He had shown me over his house. He'd got quite a fat cook—she must be a good one.

"I'm not a big eater," the priest said suddenly—could he have guessed my thoughts?

"But I drink to make up for it." He laughed.

I couldn't bring myself to laugh with him. This wine was so good, and yet I wasn't enjoying it. I wasn't talking very fluently. Why was I so shy?

"You're busy with your thoughts," came the priest's voice. "Aren't you? The children sitting in the windows painting dolls—the children who never say a word to me."

Yes, he was right.

"You're surprised that I should hear your thoughts, eh? It isn't difficult for me. The teacher here in the town is always going about with pictures of those children in his mind. We have a talk whenever we meet. You can talk in peace and comfort with me. I'm not one of those priests who turn a deaf ear, and I'm not one to grow angry. I'm at one with St. Ignatius when he said: 'I go with such a man through his door, to lead him out by mine.'"

I smiled silently while he emptied his glass. I looked at him expectantly, doubting myself.

"The cause of the distress," he continued, "doesn't lie in my taste for wine, but in the fact that the saw-mill lies idle. Our teacher here is of the opinion that with technical developments so speeded up we need new methods of production, and a totally different system of property ownership. He's right—why d'you look so surprised?"

"May I say something—rather—"

"Please."

"I think the Church always takes the side of the rich."

"Of course. The Church must."

"Must?"

"Do you know of a single state where it isn't the rich who rule? And to be rich isn't just the same thing as having money—if there were no more stock-holders in the saw-mill business, then others of the rich would rule, for a man doesn't need shares to be rich. There'll always be values, and there'll always be a few people with their hands on more of them than all the others combined. More decorations, perhaps, round their necks, more orders on their chests—whether they're on view or not—for there'll always be rich and poor, just as there'll always be the clever and the foolish. And to the Church, my dear fellow, it is not given to direct how a state should be ruled. It is the Church's duty to remain always on the side of the state—and the state, most unfortunately, will always be ruled by the rich."

"And that's the Church's duty?"

"Man is born a social animal, and so we assign him to a family, to a community or a state. The state is a man-made institution, and it only has the one goal—to produce the greatest happiness for our temporal existence. It is a necessity of nature and it is willed by God. To obey its laws is a duty to our higher selves."

"You don't wish to claim that the state we know to-day, for example, will produce the greatest happiness for all?"

"I don't claim that, for the whole of human society rests on egotism, hypocrisy, and brute force. How does Pascal put it? 'We long for the truth, and within ourselves find only uncertainty. We seek for happiness: we find misery and death.' Perhaps you are wondering how a simple country priest comes to quote Pascal. You needn't, my friend, for I can put your mind at rest there. I'm not a simple country priest: I've only been given this parish for a short time. A punitive transfer as they call it."

He smiled.

"Only very seldom," he went on, "does a man become a saint if he has never been wicked. Only very seldom do we find wisdom in one who has never been foolish. And if it weren't for the little stupidities of life, we shouldn't find ourselves in the world at all."

He laughed, with these last words—a very soft, gentle laugh, in which I couldn't bring myself to join him.

He emptied his glass once more.

"If the structure of the state is willed by God—" I began suddenly.

"Wrong. The state is a necessity of nature, and willed by God. But not the structure of the state."

"But it's the same thing!"

"No, it isn't the same thing. God created nature: what is a necessity of nature must therefore be part of the will of God. But the consequences which follow upon that creation—and here we're referring to one of them, the form of the state—is a product of man's free will. So that the state is part of the will of God, but not the structure of the state."

"And if a state collapses?"

"A state never collapses. It loses its social structure, but that only yields before another. The state itself remains, even though the people that built it may die. Another people succeeds them."

"So that the collapse of a state's structure is not a necessity of nature?"

My observation was greeted with a smile.

"Very often such a collapse is the will of God."

"Then why does the Church, when the social structure of a state is collapsing—why does the Church always take the side of the rich? To-day, for example—why is the Church always to be found supporting the share-holders in the saw-mills and not the children painting dolls in the windows?"

"Because the rich always win."

I couldn't control myself.

"A fine teaching!" I cried.

The priest went on as quietly as ever.

"Right thinking is the principle of all morality." Then, after draining his glass once again: "Yes, the rich will always win, you see they're more brutal, they're a lower type, they're more unscrupulous. We read in the Bible that a camel may pass more easily through the eye of a needle than a rich man enter the kingdom of heaven."

"And the Church? What about the Church? Will the Church pass through the eye of a needle?"

"No," came the answer—and again the smile. "That wouldn't be quite possible. For the Church is the eye of the needle."

Devilish clever, this priest, I thought to myself. But he isn't right. He isn't right.

"So the Church serves the rich, and doesn't think of fighting for the poor."

"She fights for the poor, but on another front."

"A secret front, perhaps?"

"A man may fall there too."

"Who has fallen there?"

"Jesus Christ."

"But He was God! And after Him?"

He filled my glass, pensive for a moment.

"It's a good thing," he said, "that things today in many countries, aren't going too well for the Church. It's a good thing for the Church!"

"Possibly it is," I answered abruptly, noticing how excited I had grown. "And so we come back to the children in the windows again. Didn't you say, as we were going through those streets, 'They never greet me, they hate me?' Well, you're a clever man, you ought to know that those children don't hate you at all—it's just that they've got nothing to eat."

"I think they hate me," he told me, slowly, "because they've abandoned their belief in God."

"How can you ask that of them—to believe in God?"

"God goes through every street."

"How can God go through every street—seeing those children, and doing nothing to help?"

Silently he put his glass to his lips. Then, with a grave look, he turned to me.

"God is the most terrible thing in the world."

I stared at him. I couldn't believe my ears. The most terrible?

He rose, went across to the window and looked down into the graveyard. I heard his voice again.

"God punishes," he said.

He strode up and down the room.

"We should not forget God. Even though we may not know why he is punishing us. If only we had never had our free will!"

"You mean—the doctrine of original sin?"

"Yes."

"I don't believe it."

He stopped in front of me.

"Then you can't believe in God."

"You're right. I don't believe in God."

A pause followed. I broke it, feeling I had to speak.

"Listen, I teach history, and I know that before the birth of our Lord, another world existed, the antique world—Hellas—a world without original sin—"

"I think you're in error," he murmured, going up to his book-case. He took a volume down and turned over the pages. "You're a teacher of history, so that I needn't recall to you the name of the first Greek philosopher—I mean the eldest—"

"Thales of Miletus."

"Yes. But he's a half-mythical figure, we know nothing definite about him. The first evidence of Greek philosophy that has come down to us in writing is from the hand of Anaximander—he too came from Miletus. Born 610, died 547 B.C. It amounts to only a sentence ..."

He crossed to the window again to read it, for the room was growing dark.

"'To that from which things arise must they return in the end. In pain and penance must they make good their debt for their existence, according to the universal law.'"

14. THE ROMAN CAPTAIN

WE'D BEEN FOUR DAYS IN CAMP. THE SERGEANT
had given the boys instruction in the mechanism of fire-
arms, and explained how to keep them in good working
order. To-day they spent oiling and polishing the guns
ready for target practice to-morrow.

The wooden soldiers stood ready to be hit.

The boys were in the highest spirits, though the sergeant wasn't quite so exuberant. These four days had put
ten years on his age. Another four, and he would look more
aged still. Moreover, he strained his foot, and perhaps
pulled a tendon, for he limped. However, he could grin
and bear it. I was the only one to see another side of him—
before we went to sleep the other night, he told me he'd like
to see a skittle-alley again or have a game of cards—he'd
like to be lying down in a decent bed, he'd like to hold a
buxom barmaid by the hand, he'd like—well, to be back
home. Then he went off to sleep, snoring.

He dreamed he'd become a general and won a battle.
The King had taken off all his own orders and pinned them
on his chest. And on his back. And the Queen had kissed
his feet.

"What can that mean?" he asked me next morning.

"Perhaps it was a wish-fulfilment dream." I laughed.

He told me that never in his life had he wished to have
his feet kissed by the Queen.

"I'll write to my old woman," he mused. "She's got a dream-book. She can look 'em up—General, King, Decorations, Battle, Chest, and Back. We'll find out!"

While he was writing his letter, outside the tent, up came one of the boys. It was L, and he was highly excited.

"Well, what is it?" I asked.

"I've had something stolen."

"Stolen?"

"My camera, sir—somebody's taken it."

He was quite beside himself.

The sergeant glanced up at me. He seemed to be wondering what course to take.

"Assemble everybody," I suggested. I couldn't think of anything else.

He nodded, limped to the foot of the flagpole in the centre of the camp, and bellowed the order like an old bull.

I turned to L.

"D'you suspect anybody?"

"No."

The regiment lined up. I questioned them. No one had anything to say. The sergeant and I had a look at the tent where L slept. His sleeping-bag lay just to the left of the tent flaps. We found nothing to help here.

"It seems to be out of the question," I reassured the sergeant, "that one of our own boys is the thief—in that case, we'd already have had something like this happen at school. It seems to me that the watch we've set up hasn't been too vigilant and some of that robber band have slipped through."

The sergeant thought I might be right. We decided to spend the next night supervising the sentries ourselves.

About a hundred yards away from the camp stood a

haystack. We intended to spend the night there and make it our point of vantage. The sergeant was to watch from nine till one, and I from one till six.

We slipped off after supper, escaping the notice of any of the boys. I made myself quite comfortable in the hay.

At one o'clock or thereabouts, the sergeant woke me.

"All in order so far," he whispered.

I clambered out of the hay and posted myself at the side of the rick.

The full moon cast deep shadows.

A wonderful night.

I could see the tents and distinguish the sentries. They were just changing.

To and fro, to and fro, they went; they covered the four points of the compass. Guarding their cameras!

As I sat there, I saw before me the picture in the priest's study—and in my own home.

The hours went by . . .

My school subjects are history and geography. The form of the earth, and the story of the earth—these are my province. The earth is round, but history—it struck me then—history has become a four-cornered affair . . .

I daren't smoke, for I was keeping a secret watch over the sentries . . .

My profession doesn't interest me any longer, I thought.

Why was that picture still before my mind? Was I haunted by the Crucified One? No. Or by the face of His mother? No. It was the warrior, the armed and helmeted warrior, the Roman Captain, whose face haunted me.

Why?

He conducted the execution of a Jew. And as the Jew died, he must have murmured: "There dies no man."

He had come to know God. What followed his discovery? What was his next act? He stood quiet beneath the cross. Lightning pierced the night, the curtain in the Temple was rent, the earth shuddered—the Roman Captain stood on, acknowledging the new God as the man died upon the cross—knowing that the world—his world—was condemned to death.

And then—perhaps he fell in some war. Did he know that he perished for nothing? Or perhaps he lived on into old age. Pensioned off, maybe. Was his home in Rome, or away on the frontier where living was cheaper?

A villa he might have had. A villa with a garden, and a stone dwarf. Perhaps one morning his cook told him that a new horde of barbarians was moving, beyond the frontier. Lucca, from over the way, had seen them with her own eyes.

New hordes, new peoples. Arming, arming, waiting.

That Roman Captain knew they would destroy everything. But he went on undisturbed. For him, everything had been destroyed.

And he lived on with his pension.

The mighty Roman Empire!

He had seen its frailty.

15. FILTH

THE MOON HAD RISEN HIGH OVER THE CAMP.

It must have been about two o'clock. In the city, the cafés would be crowded now. The thought of Julius Caesar passed through my mind—Julius Caesar, who'll go on flashing his death's head till the devil gets him. Funny, that—I believe in the Devil, but not in a loving God! Though I'm not sure. I think, rather, that I refuse Him my belief. With my free will.

For that's all that's left to me now, where freedom is concerned. Within myself, I can believe or refuse to believe. Before others, I must keep my views to myself. What was it the priest told me?

"It is a priest's task to prepare man for death: if a man has no fear of death, life is a less anxious thing for him."

Again:

"From this life of misery and strife, we are rescued only by the divine mercy of God, and by our belief in the Revelation."

An evasive way of putting things!

"We are punished and we do not know the reasons for our punishment."

Ask those in authority—those who rule!

But what were those last words that the priest spoke to me?

"God is the most terrible thing in the world."

Yes!

Charming were the thoughts that pierced my heart. My mind had bred them. Apparelled so becomingly, they danced along and scarcely touched the ground. A ball, a fashionable ball. In pairs they went gliding through the moonlight. Cowardice with Courage, Lies with Uprightness, Wretchedness with Strength, Malice with Valour. Only Reason and Understanding did not join in the dance. Reason and Understanding were wretchedly drunk. They had lost their virtue. But the dance went on, and I listened to the music.

A song of the streets—the song of filth.

According to language, race, or nation, we set ourselves apart, and each pile up our filth to overtower the other's.

Filth—for manure—for the earth, so that something may grow. Not flowers, but rather bread. Yes! But do not worship it—the filth of which you've eaten.

16. Z AND N

MY JOB WAS TO SIT SILENTLY IN THE SHADOW of the haystack, and keep an eye on the sentries. I was forgetting it.

I glanced round at them.

Everything in order, on all sides. But wait—something there—

The North sentry. He was talking to some one. The North sentry—Z. But I must have imagined it—the shadow of a fir-tree, nothing more.

I looked again. No shadow stood there, but a figure. At that moment the moon sailed out of a cloud. I saw a youngster—some one strange to the camp. He seemed to be giving something to Z—and then he disappeared again.

Z stood motionless for a second or two. Listening?

Cautiously he looked round before taking the letter out of his pocket. So it was a letter!

He pulled it open and read it by the moon-light. Then put it into his pocket again.

Who could be writing to Z . . . ?

Next morning, the sergeant asked me if I had seen anything worth noting. Nothing, I told him. The sentries had done their jobs properly. That was all. I didn't say a word about the letter, for I wasn't sure yet whether it had anything to do with the theft of the camera. That would come out later: I wouldn't bring Z under suspicion before anything was proved.

If only I could have read that letter!

The youngsters were quite taken aback to see us returning to camp. When had we left it?

"At midnight," lied the sergeant. "We just strolled out, but none of your sentries saw us. You want sharper eyes. With such a poor night-watch as you boys provide, anybody could sneak off with the whole camp, flags, guns, and everything that matters to us."

He then assembled the regiment, and asked if any of the boys had had his suspicions roused. He got no answer.

My eyes were on Z. He stood there, motionless as a stone. Was he carrying that letter in his pocket?

What did it say? I knew I should have to read it, that I should find myself forced to read it. Should I ask him for it straight away? No, that wouldn't do the trick. He'd lie his way out and take the first opportunity of burning the letter—and then I'd never see it.

Perhaps he'd destroyed it already.

Who could its author have been—a strange youngster who turned up in the small hours, an hour's distance away from the town? Perhaps he lived in the cottage with the old blind woman. And then it struck me, more and more forcibly, that he must belong to the robber band. The weeds.

Could Z be one of them too?

Nothing for it but to read that letter. My fingers were itching to open it. It became a fixed idea: my mind dwelled on it . . .

Boom! Boom!

I looked round: the boys were shooting for the first time.

Boom! Boom! Boom!

In the afternoon, R came up to me.

"Sir!"

"Well, R, what is it?"

"I'd like very much to sleep in another tent, sir. The two men I've got with me are scrapping the whole time, and you can't get any sleep."

"Who've you got with you?"

"N and Z."

"Z?"

"Yes, but it's always N that starts it."

"Send N to me at once."

He went, and brought back N.

"Why d'you spend your time fighting Z?" I asked him.

"Well, sir, he won't let me get to sleep. If I do, he's always waking me. He often lights his candle in the middle of the night."

"Why?"

"To write his silly trash."

"What does he write, then? Letters?"

"No! He keeps a diary, sir!"

"A diary?"

"Yes. He's—you know!"

"Why should he be on that account?"

"To keep a diary is a typical expression of egotism and conceit," he replied.

"I dare say," I answered—cautiously, for I was almost sure I'd heard this rubbish on the radio.

"Z's brought a box to keep his diary locked up in."

"Tell Z I'd like to see him."

I let N go when Z arrived.

"Why are you always fighting with N?" I asked him in his turn.

I received a startling answer.

"Because he's a plebeian."

The rich plebeians . . .

"He can't tolerate anybody being a bit introspective. It makes him mad. I keep a diary, you know—it's locked up in my box—he's been wanting to smash it lately, so I keep hiding it, sir. It's in my sleeping-bag in the day-time. At night I sleep with it."

"And where," I asked him slowly, "do you keep it when you're on sentry duty?"

"In my sleeping-bag," he replied at once.

"And in this book I take it you write up all your experiences?"

"Yes, sir."

"What you see—and hear—everything?"

He flushed.

"Yes."

Should I ask him now about the letter? No. For already my mind was made up. I would read his diary.

My eyes followed him as he left me.

Introspection—wasn't that the word he used? I'd read his very thoughts.

17. ADAM AND EVE

SOON AFTER FOUR, THE REGIMENT WAS ON THE march. The "cooks" went too this time, for the sergeant didn't want to omit anybody from his instruction. It was trenches now—how to dig them, what ground was best for dug-outs, et cetera. His sprained foot had doubled his passion for explaining things.

So that I was the only person left in the camp.

Scarcely had the regiment disappeared into the wood when I let myself into the three youngsters' tent. I found their three sleeping-bags. On one of them lay a letter— not *the* letter, of course! It was addressed to "Otto N. from (Mrs.) Elizabeth N——" the baker's wife! I couldn't resist glancing through it, to see what N's mother had written.

My dear Otto [I read]. Thanks for your p.c. Your father and I are so pleased to know you're feeling well. That's fine. But mind and see that your stockings don't get mixed up with the other boys'. So you're going to start shooting in a day or so? My Otto, shooting!—doesn't the time fly! When you start, your father says think of him, he was the best shot in his company. What do you think, Maudi died yesterday. The day before she was so playful and full of life in her cage, twittering and singing, it was beautiful. And now she's gone—I don't know what it was, some illness canaries get. Her little legs were so limp. I burned her up in the fire. Yesterday we had a lovely piece of venison, and cranberries. We thought of you. Do they feed you well? Father sends you his love, he says always tell him if your teacher says anything else like he did about the niggers, and he'll break his neck. Well, Otto, my dear, we both send you our love. Good-bye. Your loving mother.

The next sleeping-bag held nothing hidden. This was R's. So the box must be inside the third: and then I found it. A thin bluish metal box with a very simple lock. I'd have to try it with a piece of wire.

I was soon successful.

Inside lay letters, postcards, and a book bound in green leather. "MY DIARY" was printed on the cover in gilt lettering. On the fly-leaf there was an inscription:

"From Mummy. Christmas 193—."

Who was Z's mother? Some official's wife—or widow, I seemed to remember.

The first entries Z had made were about a Christmas-tree. I turned over a few pages and came to Easter. In this first section, something had been written every day, but later, only every other day, and then at intervals—every fifth or sixth. Suddenly I came upon the letter.

A crumpled envelope. No stamp, no address.

Now to read it, at last! Quickly!

"Can't come to-day. To-morrow at two. —EVE."

Just that.

Eve? I know who Adam was—Z.

And now I had to peep into the diary.

Wednesday.

Arrived at the camp yesterday. Everything very jolly. It's evening now, couldn't get down to write yesterday, everybody fagged out with putting up tents. We've got a flag too—and an old fool of a sergeant who can't see when we're taking the rise out of him—we're quicker. Thank the lord we hardly ever see our form-master. He's always going about with a doleful face, and he doesn't care two hoots about us. N's another fool. Now he's yelling at me for the second time to put out the candle, but I'm not having any or I'd never get this diary filled in and I want memories for my life. This afternoon we did a super march, right to the foot of the mountains. On the way we came across cliffs with a number of holes in them—caves. All at once the sergeant raps out an order, spread out and advance through the brush towards an imaginary enemy, which he pointed out to us hidden behind a ridge and armed with heavy machine-guns. We spread out, leaving a pretty good space between each of us, but the brushwood grew thicker and thicker and soon I couldn't see right or left, I was cut off, I'd lost my bearings. Then I came to one of the cliffs, with a cave in it. I think I must have gone round in a circle—and there was a girl standing in front of me. A darkish blonde with a red blouse. Where the dickens could she have sprung from? She asked me who I was. I told her. She had two chaps with her about my age, both barefooted and very ragged. They didn't look too friendly. The girl told them they could go, and she'd show me the way back through the brush. I was jolly glad. She came with me. I asked her where she lived and she told me, in the cliffs. But on the Army map I had there was no house marked round here anywhere. The map's wrong, I thought. We came to the edge of the brushwood and I caught a glimpse of the camp in the distance. She stopped and said she must turn back now and she'd give me a kiss if I wouldn't tell a soul I'd seen her. Why? I asked her. Because she didn't want it known, she said. I told her that was all right, and she gave me a kiss on the cheek. That wouldn't do, I told her, a kiss is only a kiss on the lips. She did it and put her tongue in my mouth. I told her she was a pig, what did she mean by that. She laughed and gave me another one. I pushed her off. She picked up a stone and threw it at me. If it had caught me on the head—! I told her she might have done for me. She said that wouldn't trouble her. They'd hang you, though, I said. She said it wouldn't matter much. Suddenly I felt—well, scared. She told me to come near her. I didn't want to be a coward, I went. She suddenly took hold of me and kissed me again, with her tongue in my mouth. I got furious. I grabbed a branch and laid into her. I struck her on the back and on the shoulders, but not on the head. She didn't scream or anything. She collapsed. There she was lying on the ground. I was terrified. I thought she might be dead! I went up to her and touched her with the branch. She didn't move. She just lay there as if she were done for. I wanted to run, but then I saw through her game—she was pretending. Her eyes were blinking up at me. I went near her again. She wasn't dead. I've seen a few dead

people, and they look quite different. When I was
seven, I saw a dead policeman and four workers.
Some strike was on. You wait, I thought! You wanted
to give me a start, but you were too quick. I gently
slid my hands under her coat and then pushed it
up. She had no knickers on. Still she kept as quiet
as a mouse—but not I, by now. Then suddenly she
jerked herself up and pulled me down on her madly.
We made love. Just near by was a huge ant-heap.
After, I promised I'd tell nobody I'd seen her. She ran
off then. I forgot to ask her her name.

Thursday.

We've got the sentries out now against the robber
band. There goes N, yelling again for me to put the
candle out. If he does it again, I'll give him one to
remember. I have already. He didn't hit back. That
fool R yelled out, just as if he'd caught it himself. I'm
mad I didn't make a date with that girl. I'd like to
have seen her again and spoken to her. This morning, when the sergeant was taking our exercises,
I could still feel her against me. I think of her the
whole time. It's only her tongue I don't like. But she
told me you grow into doing that—like speeding
when you drive a car—I think it must be something
like flying. But flying must be more marvellous still.
It's very solitary, I wish she were here. I don't think
I'd mind if she put her tongue in my mouth.

Friday.

The day after to-morrow we're going to shoot. At
last. This afternoon, had a scrap with N. I'll finish

him. R got some of it too. What does the idiot want to stand in the way for? But what's all that to me? I just think of her all the time, more and more. Last night she came. Just like that, when I was on sentry duty. I was rather scared at first, then I felt fine and was ashamed of being scared. Thank the Lord she didn't see I was. She smelled of a wonderful perfume. When I asked her how she got it, she said she'd got it in the town, at the chemist's. I said it must have been jolly dear. Oh, no, she said, it didn't cost her anything. Then she put her arms round me again. She asked me, What now. I said we'd make love. Should we often, she asked. Yes, I said. Did I think she was a bad girl? No, how could she say that. Because she'd come to me at night. No girl's a saint, I told her. Then suddenly I saw a tear on her cheek, the moon was shining on her face. I asked her why she was crying. She said because everything looked so gloomy. How did she mean? Then she asked me if I'd love her if she were a lost soul. She said she'd got no parents. When she was twelve she'd got a job as a maid, but the master was always running after her. She'd tried to keep to herself. Then she'd stolen some money to run away, because her mistress was always boxing her ears because of her husband—then she was put in an institution but she escaped and now she lived in a cave and meant to steal everything she could. Four chaps from the town, who'd got tired of painting dolls, were with her, but she was the eldest and the leader. But I wasn't to tell anybody she was one of them, for then she'd have to go back to the reformatory. She quite upset me and I suddenly felt she must have a soul. I told her so. She said yes, she was sure, too, that she had a soul. But I mustn't give her away if while she was with me anything disappeared from the camp. I told her I'd never give her away, we belonged to each other. It's only me you mustn't steal from, I said. Then we had to part, as I should soon be relieved. To-morrow we're meeting again. I know her name now. Eve.

Saturday.

Great commotion to-day. L's had his camera stolen. What's the odds? His father's got three factories, poor Eve's got to live in a cave. What'll she do when it's winter? There's N yelling about the light again. I'll kill him.

I can scarcely wait for the night she comes. I'd like to live in a tent with her, but no camp, all alone. Nobody but her. I'm sick of the camp. Sick of it.

I'll always be ready for you, Eve, waiting! They shan't put you back in any reformatory, I swear it. I'll defend you always.

There's N again—he's going to smash up my box to-morrow, just let him try it once. I keep my deepest secrets in it, they're for me alone. Whoever touches my box shall die.

18. CONDEMNED

"WHOEVER TOUCHES MY BOX SHALL DIE."

I read this last phrase again and I had to smile. Just like boys.

I was reflecting on what I'd read, but my reflections didn't have time to amount to very much. I heard the bugle from the fringe of the wood. The regiment was nearly home: I must hurry. I slipped the diary back into the box and tried to lock it. I turned the wire this way and that. No good. It wouldn't click. I'd broken the lock.

They'd be back in a moment now. I put the box, still unlocked, back into the sleeping-bag and left the tent. There was nothing else for it. The regiment had returned.

Z was marching in the fourth row.

You've got a girl now, Z, called Eve. And you know your beloved is a thief, and yet you swear you'll defend her to the last.

I smiled again. These boys!

The regiment halted and dismissed . . .

And now your innermost thoughts are familiar things to me, I thought. But I couldn't smile any longer. For I saw the case coming into court—the public prosecutor going over his notes: an indictment for theft and connivance at theft. Adam would have to answer questions, besides Eve. Z would be arrested.

I ought to tell the sergeant and notify the police—or should I have a talk with Z alone first?

He had gone over to the kitchen quarters to see what there was for supper. He'd have to leave the high school and the girl would be sent back to an institution.

Or prison—for both. Good-bye to your fair future, Z.

Better men than you have found a stumbling-block in love, that is a necessity of nature, and hence willed by God.

I heard the priest's words again: "God is the most terrible thing in the world"—and another sound fell on my ears—a terrific up-roar of shouting and screaming. Every one was rushing to one of the tents—the tent that housed that box. Z and N were fighting so savagely that the others could hardly tear them apart. N's face was smeared with blood from his broken lips. Z's was blanched with fury.

"N's broken his box open!" the sergeant shouted over to me.

"I didn't!" yelled N. "I didn't, it wasn't me."

"Who else was it, then?" shouted Z. "Who could it have been, sir, if it wasn't N?"

"Liar!"

"He did it. Nobody else would. He always threatened he'd smash it open."

"But I didn't—"

"Quiet!" roared the sergeant.

Quiet came suddenly.

Z's eyes had never left N. Whoever broke open his box should die. As I remembered that last entry of his, involuntarily I looked upwards.

There was no storm in that soft sky.

Yes, Z could kill N, I was sure. As if N was thinking the same thing, he turned, a little frightened, to me.

"Sir, I'd like to sleep in another tent."

"Very well."

"Really, sir, I haven't read it—I haven't read his diary. Help me to prove it, sir!"

"I'll do all I can for you."

Z glanced at me. How can you help him, his glance seemed to say. For I knew. I had doomed N.

But still I wanted to know if Z himself took part in the thieving. I didn't want to throw suspicion on him without cause—and it was I who had broken that lock.

Why didn't I tell him that it was I who had read his diary?

No, not yet. Not there and then, in front of everybody. I couldn't. I'd be too ashamed. Later, yes, but not yet.

I'd tell him when we were alone. And I'd have a talk with the girl too, to-night, when he met her. I'd tell her never to show her face again, and I'd give Z a pretty straight talking to. And that would be the end of the whole thing.

Guilt, like a vulture, hovers over us, ready to swoop.

But I'd absolve N. He should be right out of this. He'd done nothing. And I'd pardon Z and the girl too. I wouldn't let myself be doomed for nothing.

God might be terrible, but I, with my free will, would frustrate His plans, I'd save all of us. In the midst of my thoughts, I felt that someone's eyes were staring at me.

T's—two glazed, round eyes, still and lustreless.

The Fish—the Age of the Fish. I'd seen them at the funeral of little W.

And T seemed to smile—quietly, scornfully. A fixed, mocking smile. Did he know that my hand had broken that lock?

19. THE MAN IN THE MOON

THE DAY WORE ON SLOWLY.

Sundown came at last.

In the twilight, I waited for night; and as night fell, I slipped out of the camp. The sergeant was snoring already. Not a soul had seen me go. The dull moon hung over the tents. From the western sky drifted dark, ragged clouds— and then for longer and longer intervals the silver light was obscured.

Z's post lay on the north, where the wood and the camp almost touched. I took up my position there, under a tree.

I could make out the sentry from here—it was G. Z's turn had not come.

G paced up and down.

The clouds swept over the sky; but here, on the earth, nothing stirred. Only a bough creaked now and then. Then G would prick up his ears and stare into the wood. Frightened? A wood was never quite still, least of all at night.

Minutes passed—and I saw Z. He muttered a word to G, who left his post. Z was alone. He looked up at the moon. His eyes were full of caution.

Perhaps there was a man in the moon, sitting up there in his circle of yellow light, smoking his pipe, without a care in the world—and spitting down on us.

The girl showed up at last, at half-past two or

thereabouts. She came so soundlessly that I wasn't aware of her till she stood at Z's side. She seemed to appear from nowhere. They embraced and kissed. The girl had her back towards me. Z I could not see. She must be taller than he.

Very quietly I got up, to go over and speak to them. If the girl heard me, she'd run off. And I had to have a word with her.

They were still in each other's arms.

They're weeds, I thought, they ought to be rooted up—I heard the old peasant's words again: and I saw that old blind stumbling woman—and the girl, stretching and peeping over the hedge. She must have a beautiful back. I'd like to see her eyes too . . .

A cloud suddenly darkened the moon—a little cloud, hemmed with silver light as it passed.

I started to go over to the couple. Then I saw that the girl had taken off her clothes. Z was kneeling before her.

How white she was!

I waited. She seemed lovelier to me.

Go on! Tell them it was you who broke that lock. You, and not N . . .

But I had come to a standstill. Z was sitting on a tree-trunk, the girl on his knees. Her legs were strong and beautiful.

While I still lingered, another cloud, deeper and heavier, came up, and no silver hem rimmed it as it passed. The earth was darkened. The sky was darkened. I could see nothing.

I listened. Steps through the wood?

I held my breath.

Steps? Or only the storm, up there in the sky? Every-thing was black as pitch before me. Where are you, Adam and Eve? By the sweat of your brow must you earn your bread—but you haven't thought of that, have you? Eve steals cameras, Adam winks his eyes while he should be on guard. I'll tell him to-morrow, early to-morrow, who broke open his box. To-morrow. I'll let nothing stand in my way—even if God should send me a thousand naked forms . . .

The darkness grew even deeper. I was held close by the still, sooty night.

I must go back now.

I pushed out a groping hand. And touched a tree.

I drew back—groped again, and shuddered: I'd felt something. My heart stopped.

I wanted to cry out, but took hold of myself.

My outstretched hand had felt not a tree, but a face.

What lay before me? I stood, not daring to move.

A delusion?

No, I'd touched a nose, and lips.

I sat down on the ground. Wait for that cloud to pass! Don't move!

And up there beyond the clouds, the man in the moon smoked his pipe. A few raindrops fell.

Spit down on me from your yellow world!

20. THE LAST DAY BUT ONE

MORNING AT LAST, GREY AND PALE.

There was no one before me. The face had gone. I slipped back to the camp. The sergeant lay snoring on his back with his mouth open. Rain pattered on the canvas. For the first time in hours, I felt tired. I fell hungrily asleep.

The regiment had gone before I woke. As soon as Z came back I'd tell him it was I, not N.

It was the last day here but one. To-morrow we'd be striking camp and driving back to the city.

It rained in torrents now—sharp torrents that abated now and then. Clouds of mist hung in the valleys. We shouldn't see the mountains again.

At midday the boys returned.

But with one missing—N.

He must have lost his way, the sergeant thought—he'd soon turn up. I thought of the caves that Z had described in his diary. I frowned.

Fear?

I must tell him now.

He was sitting in his tent, writing. Alone. At my approach he quickly hid his diary. He looked up at me suspiciously.

"So we're keeping our diary up?" I tried to smile.

He glowered at me in silence. I noticed that his hands

were scratched. He saw me observe them. He started, and put them in his pockets.

"Cold?" I muttered, my eyes on his.

He only nodded. His lips twisted into a wry smile.

"Listen," I began slowly. "You think it was N who broke open your box?"

"I don't think, I know. Who else could it have been?"

"How do you know?"

"He told me."

N had told him? Himself? But that was impossible. He couldn't have.

Z's eyes seemed to pierce me now. After a moment, he went on:

"He admitted it this morning—that it was he who broke open the box. With a piece of wire. He couldn't shut it again. He'd broken the lock."

"Well?"

"He asked me to forgive him. I did."

"You forgave him?"

"Yes, sir."

Now he wore an air of indifference. That last entry in his diary recurred to me.

Absurd, though.

Z was calm enough.

"Where's N now—do you know?" I asked.

"How should I know, sir? I expect he lost his way. I've done it once or twice."

He got up, as if he didn't want to talk any more.

I noticed now that his coat was torn . . .

Should I tell him that he was lying? That N had never made such a confession—because it was I who had read the diary? But why was Z lying?

No, I mustn't think of that—

Why couldn't I have told him the truth straight away, when he was scrapping with N? Because I was ashamed of confessing before my own pupils that I'd picked that lock in secret, with a piece of wire—although it was with the best of intentions? Of course! Why had I overslept that morning? And I'd spent the night in the wood, without saying a word.

And now there was no point in saying anything.

It was too late. And I was the stone over which he had stumbled, the pit into which he had fallen, the cliff from which he was hurled down—oh, why could no one have wakened me earlier this morning? I didn't want guilt to fall on me unawares. But I slept instead of vindicating myself. With my free will I'd wanted to frustrate those plans. But they had been made too long. I wanted to rescue all of us, but we were beyond aid—drowned, in the eternal sea of guilt. Whose fault was it that that lock had broken? That it wouldn't shut to? Yet even if it had, I should still have spoken up.

The paths of guilt cross each other and intertwine. A maze, a labyrinth—with distorting mirrors at every corner.

A fairground.

Step this way, everybody, step this way!

With penance and with pain, redeem the guilt of your life.

I need have no anxiety now. It was too late . . .

In the afternoon, we all set out in search of N. We combed the whole neighbourhood, shouting his name ceaselessly. But no answer came. I wasn't expecting an answer.

Twilight fell. We turned back. Soaked to the skin, and frozen—and to no avail.

"If it keeps coming down like this," cursed the sergeant, "there'll be such a lovely flood."

When the rains ceased and the waters of the flood receded, the Lord spoke. "I will not again curse the ground any more for man's sake."

Had the Lord God kept that promise?

The rain fell heavier. I heard the sergeant's voice.

"We'll have to notify the police that N's missing."

"To-morrow."

"I can't understand you. It doesn't seem to bother you at all."

"I should think he's got lost—it's easily done, after all. He may be staying the night at some cottage."

"Unfortunately there aren't any cottages round here. Only caves."

The word struck me like a blow.

"Anyway, let's hope he's found his way into one of them and hasn't broken any bones."

"Yes, let's hope—"

On an impulse, I asked a question.

"Why didn't you wake me earlier this morning?"

"Didn't wake you?" He laughed. "Why didn't I wake you! I had a shot, but you just slept on as if the devil had got hold of you."

God is the most terrible thing in the world.

21. THE LAST DAY

ON THE LAST DAY OF OUR CAMP CAME GOD.

His coming did not take me by surprise.

The sergeant and the boys were taking down the tents when He came.

He brought terror. The sergeant felt his strength ebbing away and had to rest. The boys stood clustered around him, half paralysed with fear. Then slowly he got to work again, troubled and excited.

Only Z's movements were still calm. He strolled to and fro—to and fro—to and fro.

And then from every one a great shriek rang out—or so it seemed to me. Only Z kept silent.

Two men had come into the camp, woodsmen with their bags, their saws, and their axes. They'd found one of our boys, his school-papers were still on him. It was N.

They found him near the caves, in a ditch close to a clearing. There was a gaping wound in his head.

He must have been struck by a stone or some blunt instrument. When they found him he was quite dead.

I went down to the town with the woodsmen. We almost ran.

Struck with a stone—

At the camp, the shadow of God remained.

The police got into communication with the Public

Prosecutor in the nearest big city and I sent a telegram to my head master.

A number of policemen were detailed to go to the scene of the crime.

There lay N in the ditch, face forward.

His photograph was taken. A thorough search was made for the stone or instrument that had struck him, and any clues that could be detected.

It was discovered that N had not been struck in the spot where he lay, but at a distance of twenty yards or so. There were clear traces of his having been dragged over the ground to the ditch where the body had been hidden.

The stone came to light, too. A jagged stone, flecked with blood. A pencil was also found—and a compass.

The doctor was able to state that the stone had struck N's head with enormous force, the blow coming from very close at hand—probably from behind him.

Was N running away?

A considerable struggle must have preceded the deed, for his coat was torn.

And his hands scratched . . .

We went to the camp next, and I saw Z. He was sitting down, rather aloof from his fellows. I thought of his coat. And his hands. I must be on my guard: I didn't want to let that slip out. My coat wasn't torn, and there were no scratches on my hands, but my guilt remained.

An examination followed. No one could furnish any information about the crime. I said nothing. Z said nothing.

I was asked if I had any suspicions—and again I saw God. I saw Him beside Z's tent. The diary was in His hand. Then, in my picture, He spoke to R, but his eyes were all the while on Z. Little R seemed not to see God, but to hear

Him none the less. His eyes opened wide: he had looked into an unearthly realm.

They were questioning me again.

"Well? Is there anyone you suspect?"

"No."

"Sir, sir!" little R cried suddenly, pressing his way forward to the Public Prosecutor. "Z and N were always fighting. N read Z's diary and so Z hated him, like an enemy—he keeps a diary locked up in a steel box!"

All eyes turned to Z.

His head hung bowed. We couldn't see his face. Had he flushed, or blanched?

Slowly he came forward.

The stillness was very tense.

"Yes," he said quietly. "I did it."

He cried.

Another picture came into my mind. In it, God smiled. Why?

His image faded as I asked.

22. THE PRESSMEN

TO-MORROW—THE TRIAL.

I was sitting in a café-terrace, reading the papers. The evening was chilly. Autumn had come.

For a week already the papers had been headlining the murder. In some of them it was "The Z Case," in others "The N Case"; and their columns were full of comments and sketches. Cases with any similar aspect were unearthed and written up, various opinions were expressed of modern youth in general and in particular, different theories poured in, and every line of it directly or indirectly led back to the murdered N and his assailant, Z.

That morning, a reporter had come to me for an interview. It must be in print by now, in the evening edition. I bought one—and discovered that I had been photographed. Yes, that was my picture—though I could scarcely recognize myself. Beneath it I read: "What does the Teacher think?"

Well, what?

… From our own Correspondent.
This morning, at the high school, I obtained an interview with the teacher who last spring was in charge of the camping-unit in which the crime occurred.

The teacher told me that he is still as baffled as ever
by this terrible tragedy of youth. Z, he informed me,
was always one of the brightest of his pupils: he had
never noticed traces of abnormality in his character,
and certainly nothing suggestive of mental defects
or criminal instincts. I then put a grave question to
him: was it possible that this crime had its origin
in a certain brutalization of our youth? The teacher
waved my theory aside.

"The youth of to-day," he explained, "bears no
traces of brutalization. Thanks to a high standard
of health, our youngsters have a strong sense of de-
votion to duty and they place their country before
themselves. This murder is a solitary and deeply re-
grettable example of retrogression to the worst days
of liberalism."

The bell rang; break was over, and the teacher
had to go back to his class and his task of building
up his young material into worthy patriots. It is indeed something to be thankful for that this murder
case represents only an exceptionally rare outbreak
of criminal individualism.

An interview with the sergeant was printed below
mine. There was a picture of him too, as he might have
looked thirty years ago, the conceited fool.

What had he to say?

I then spent a few minutes with the Military Instruction Chief—or, in short, the I.C. He greeted
me with the greatest courtesy and in his bearing I
was aware of the vigour of an old soldier who has

never let himself grow stale. In his view, the tragedy
is due to a lack of discipline. He had a few words to
say about the condition of the corpse when it was
found. He had been through the whole of the last
war and had never seen such a grisly wound. "As an
old soldier, I'm all for peace," he said in conclusion
of this revelatory interview.

I also saw the President of the Society for the
Prevention of Neglect and Cruelty to Children,
Mrs. K, who is the wife of a master chimney-sweep.
She bitterly deplored the case. For days, she stated,
she has been troubled by disturbing dreams. In her
opinion, it is high time that better schools of cor-
rection were established, in view of the social need
for them.

I turned over the page. Who was this? I was right. It was
the baker, N, the murdered boy's father. His wife's picture
was there too. Mrs. Elizabeth N, *née* S——.

"I will readily answer your questions," said the baker
to me. "Incorruptible justice will elicit whether our
poor Otto fell victim to the unpardonable negli-
gence of those in charge of him. I am thinking of
the teacher in this connection—the thought of the
I.C. does not enter my head. *Justitia Fundamentum
Regnorum.* The teachers in our schools should be
subjected to a severe examination: they form a body
which still swarms with corrupt enemies to the
State's interests."

"Otto was my son," said Mrs. N. "Now I have
only my husband. But little Otto and I are still in

spiritual contact with each other. I belong to a spiritualist circle."

On another page I found the following:

The boy-murderer's mother occupies a small, three-roomed apartment. She is the widow of a University professor, who died about ten years ago. Professor Z was a noted physiologist. His study of the reaction of the nerves during amputations excited much comment, even beyond the bounds of the medical profession. Some twenty years ago he was for a period the target of an attack by a society of anti-vivisectionists. Mrs. Z would make no comment on the case. "Gentlemen," she said, "you must see how upset I am." A lady of middle height, she was in mourning.

In a third paper I encountered the Counsel for the Defence. I had already spoken to him two or three times and I knew that he was putting heart and soul into the case: as a young lawyer, with his way to make, he was well aware of what it meant to him.

He was in the limelight. Here was a long interview.

"In this sensational case of murder, gentlemen," he began, "the defence is clearly in a precarious position. What we have to fight is not only the prosecution, but also the accused, whom we are supposed to defend."

"In what way?"

"The accused, gentlemen, has confessed to a

criminal attack on the dead boy. I want you to realize particularly that manslaughter, and not murder, is involved. But in spite of the confession we have had from the young person, I am profoundly convinced that he is not responsible for this deed. To my mind, he is shielding another party."

"You don't wish to assert, Doctor—that the crime was committed by some one else?"

"But, gentlemen, that is exactly what I do assert. And further—quite apart from what my intuition tells me, an intuition sharpened by the practice of criminal law—I have certain very definite grounds for my assertion. The boy Z was not the culprit. Consider the motive for a moment. Here we have a schoolboy killing his class-mate, because the latter read his diary. But what did this diary contain? Little else besides an account of the affair with this wanton girl. He is shielding the girl, and he writes thoughtlessly, 'Whoever touches this diary shall die.' Yes, I know, everything looks unfavourable—and yet not quite everything, gentlemen! Apart from the fact that his confession, in every way, sounds a certain note of chivalry—quite apart from that, isn't it rather remarkable that he hasn't said a word about the actual deed? Not a word! And why will he tell us nothing? He says he cannot remember! I think otherwise. He had not the remotest idea as to where, when, or how this poor class-mate was done to death—that's why he couldn't remember! All he knows is that the instrument used was a stone. We show him the stone—and still he can't recall anything! Gentlemen, he is shielding another party!"

"But his torn coat—and the scratches on his hands?"

"Admittedly, he encountered N by the cliffs and they had a fight—that much he has described to us in detail! But did he, afterwards, follow him stealthily and hit him from behind with a stone? Oh, no! It was another who raised that stone: a girl."

"The girl already implicated?"

"Yes, she dominated him, she still dominates him. He is under her spell. Gentlemen, we are going to call in psychiatrists."

"Will the girl be called as a witness?"

"Of course. Shortly after the crime, she was arrested in one of the caves. She and her gang have been in custody for some time now. Yes, we shall hear what Eve has to say—perhaps to-morrow."

"How long do you think the trial will last?"

"I consider it likely to last two or three days. Few witnesses will be called, but, as I have said, I have to face a sharp contest with the accused. I intend to fight it through to the end. The boy Z will receive a sentence for aiding and abetting theft—nothing more."

Nothing more.
No one has brought God into it.

23. THE TRIAL

AT THE DOORS OF THE COURT STOOD A CROWD three hundred strong—the doors were closed, but all still sought admission: the passes had been exhausted weeks before. A good many wires had been pulled to obtain them, but the control now was very strict.

The corridors were full. Everybody had come for a glimpse of Z, and fashionable women were in the forefront. To these blasé and sensual creatures, the disaster afforded the fervour of sensual pleasure undiminished by fears of pregnancy to follow. The catastrophe of others was their bedmate. It engendered an artificial sympathy in which they took their delicate delight.

The Press gallery was thronged.

The witnesses were N's parents, Z's mother, the sergeant, the boy R who had shared the tent with Z and N, the two woodsmen who had discovered the body, the policemen and other officials. And of course, myself—and Eve.

But she was not present yet. She would be brought in later.

Counsel for the Prosecution and Counsel for the Defence were going through their notes. While Eve remained solitary in her cell, waiting.

The accused was brought in by a policeman.

He had changed little. His face was paler and his eyes

blinked, as if the light were too strong. His hair was neatly brushed.

In the dock, he looked as if he were sitting at his desk in school. All eyes were on him. He looked up shyly, and caught sight of his mother.

What did he feel that impelled him to stare at her like that? In answer, his mother scarcely glanced back—or was that only my mistaken impression? She was so heavily veiled. Folds of black lace—that was all I could see.

The sergeant nodded to me and asked if I'd read his interview in the papers.

"Yes," I answered. The baker N heard my voice with hatred in his face.

He would like to strike me dead—with one of his stale rolls, perhaps.

24. A VEIL

EVERY ONE ROSE AS THE PRESIDENT OF THE Juvenile Court marched up the room. He sat down to open the case.

A nice old grandpa, he looked.

The indictment was read. Z was accused not of manslaughter but murder—murder with malice aforethought.

Grandpa nodded, as if to say, "Oh, these children!" Then he turned to the dock. Z rose.

He gave his name and age in a clear, unstrained voice. He was asked to give an account of his life, and to speak freely. With a furtive glance towards his mother, he began.

He had been brought up in the same way as most children. His parents had not been over strict. His father had died a long time ago. He was an only child.

His mother touched her veiled eyes with her handkerchief as her son quietly went on to tell the court of his early ambitions. He wanted to be a great inventor. But he didn't want to invent mere "gadgets" like a new zipp-fastener.

"That sounds very sensible," agreed the President. "But what if you'd found you couldn't invent anything?"

"Then I'd have been a pilot. In the air-mail service. An overseas pilot, that's what I'd have liked best."

Flying to the negroes? My thoughts still sped involuntarily towards them.

And as Z went on speaking of his lost career, the time drew nearer and nearer—soon he would be approaching the day when God came.

He gave us a picture of life in the camp, with the shooting and marching, the hoisting of the colours. He mentioned the sergeant, and he mentioned me: and here he said a strange thing.

"Our teacher's opinions often seemed to me very childish ones."

The President was astonished.

"What do you mean?"

"He was always telling us how things should be in this world, and not how they really are."

The President looked very gravely down at Z. Did he feel that the accused's recital was beginning to touch upon a sphere which the radio ruled? Where the urge for decency is relegated to the scrap-heap while man grovels in the dust before the brutality of things as they exist? Yes, that was his fear—for he took the first opportunity that came to leave this dubious subject for a higher and more nebulous one.

"Do you believe in God?" he asked.

"Yes," answered Z, without a pause.

"And you know the fifth commandment?"

"Yes, sir."

"Are you sorry for what you have done?"

The room was very still.

"Yes," said Z, "very sorry."

But his sorrow did not ring true.

The President blew his nose.

Z was now coming to the day of the murder; the details, which every one knew by heart, were gone over once more.

"We marched off very early that morning," Z explained for the hundredth time. "And soon we spread out over the bushes to advance on a chain of hills held by an imaginary enemy. Near the caves I ran up against N. We were on one of the rocky parts. I was mad with him because he broke open my box, though he denied it—"

"Stop!" ordered the President. "Your teacher made a statement to the local magistrate to the effect that you told him that N had admitted to breaking open the box."

"I only said that, sir."

"Why?"

"So that nobody should start suspecting me when it came out."

"Aha! Go on."

"We started to fight, N and I, and he almost threw me down off the rocks. I saw red. I sprang back and threw the stone at him."

"You were still on the rock?"

"No—"

"Where, then?"

"I've—forgotten."

He smiled. It seemed impossible to drag anything further from him. He didn't remember.

"Well, where does your memory pick up again?" was the President's next question.

"I went back to the camp and wrote in my diary that I'd had a fight with N."

"Yes, that is the last entry. But you left that closing sentence unfinished."

"The teacher interrupted me."

"What did he wish to see you for?"

"I don't know, sir."

"Well, no doubt he'll tell us."

On the table in the court-room lay the diary, a pencil, and a compass. And a stone.

The President inquired whether Z recognized the stone.

"Yes." He nodded.

"And to whom does the pencil belong—and this compass?"

"They don't belong to me."

"They belonged to poor N," said the President, glancing at his notes. "No—wait—only the pencil belonged to N. Why didn't you say that the compass belonged to you?"

Z blushed.

"I forgot," he murmured.

Z's counsel rose.

"Perhaps the compass really doesn't belong to him, your honour."

"What do you imply by that?"

"I wish to imply that this fatal compass, which wasn't N's property, might not have been Z's either, but might have belonged to a third person. Would your honour be so good as to ask the accused if there was not actually a third person on the scene?"

He sat down again. Z threw him a baleful look.

"There was no third person there," he said firmly.

The defence sprang up at that.

"How is it that he remembers that fact so definitely when he has quite forgotten how, when, and where the crime took place?"

The prosecuting lawyer too had now got to his feet. His tone was full of irony.

"Apparently my learned friend wishes to infer that it

was not the accused who committed the murder, but a
Mysterious Unknown—"

"Isn't there"—the defence turned to him—"isn't there a
certain wanton girl, the leader of a robber band, to be con-
sidered? Even supposing there is no further element, she
can hardly be labelled a Mysterious Unknown."

"It wasn't the girl. She's been sufficiently questioned,
in all conscience. We shall hear what the magistrate who
examined her has to say. Let alone the fact that the accused
made a very plain confession—and the fact that he made it
without delay speaks somewhat in his favour. The attempt
on the part of the defence to make it appear that the girl
committed the crime, and that the accused is shielding her,
is on the verge of being fantastic."

"The case isn't finished yet," smiled the defence. He
turned to Z.

"I see there is an entry in your diary which reads, 'She
took a stone and threw it at me—and if it had hit me, I
shouldn't be here now.'"

Z quietly met his gaze. Then, with a negative gesture:

"I was exaggerating. It was only a small stone."

Suddenly a tremor shook him.

"Don't defend me, sir. I want to be punished for what
I've done."

"And what about your mother?" cried his counsel.
"Have you thought of your mother, and what she's suffering? You aren't aware of the harm you're doing."

Z lowered his head.

Then—searchingly, almost—he glanced at his mother.

She was the object of every eye. But none could pierce
those heavy veils.

25. HIS DWELLING

BEFORE THE WITNESSES WERE CALLED, THE court adjourned for lunch.

It was midday. Slowly the court-room emptied. The accused was led away. Defending and prosecuting counsel exchanged glances equally confident of victory.

I went out for a stroll in the gardens surrounding the Law Courts.

A dreary day, dank and cold.

Leaves falling—yes, it was autumn now.

Turning a corner, I stopped short. For a moment. Then I went on.

On one of the benches sat a still figure. Z's mother.

I noticed that she was a woman of medium height.

My automatic greeting was not returned.

She did not seem to see me.

She seemed far away.

The time is past now when I believed there was no God.

To-day I believe in Him. I can still see Him as I saw Him in the camp, when He spoke to little R and gazed at Z.

His eyes must be piercing, cruel, and cold, very cold. No. He is not a good God.

Why does He let Z's mother sit there like that? What has she done? Can the guilt of her son's crime be laid at her feet? Why does He condemn the mother, if He damns the son? No, it is not just . . .

I felt in my pockets for my cigarettes.

Silly of me, I must have left them at home.

I left the gardens and went in search of a tobacconist's.

I found one in a side street. A tiny shop kept by a very old couple. It took a long time for the old man to open the packet and for his wife to count out ten cigarettes. They got in each other's way, but took it all with a kindly good humour.

The old woman gave me too little change, and when I brought it smilingly to her notice, she cried out in alarm:

"God preserve us!"

If God preserves you, I thought, then you are indeed secure.

She had no more small change and went across to the butcher's to get some.

I stayed behind with the old man and lit a cigarette.

He asked whether I were from the Law Courts. Most of his customers were legal gentlemen. And he began to talk about the murder trial: it was a strange and most interesting case, this, for you could clearly see the hand of God at work in it.

I looked up quickly.

The hand of God?

"Yes," he went on, "for every one connected with the case seems to be guilty. Even the witnesses, the sergeant, the teacher—and the parents too!"

"The parents?"

"Yes. It's not only the young people—their parents as well don't trouble about God nowadays. They act as if He didn't exist."

I looked out onto the street. The old woman came out of the butcher's shop and turned right towards the baker's. So the butcher had no change either!

The street was empty. And I was troubled by a sudden disturbing thought: it was not by mere chance that the butcher had no change. Chance alone did not keep me waiting here.

I looked up at the tall grey houses.

"If only one knew where God lives!" I said.

"He lives everywhere—everywhere where He is not forgotten," came the old man's reply. "He dwells here with us, that's why we never quarrel!"

I caught my breath.

What was that?

Still the voice of the old man?

No, not his, but another voice.

Who was speaking to me?

I did not turn my head.

Again the voice came:

"When you are called as witness and name my name in the oath, do not conceal the fact that it was you who broke open the box."

The box!

No, for then I shall only be punished because I shielded the thief.

"Do this!"

But I shall lose my work, my daily bread.

"Then you must lose it, rather than bring about a new injustice!"

But my parents? I am their only support.

"Shall I show you your childhood?"

My childhood?

My scolding mother, my angry father, for ever quarrel-
ling. No, You did not dwell here, You only passed by—Your
coming brought no joy...

I was close to tears.

"Tell them," the voice came once more. "Tell them it
was you who broke open the box. Do my will and grieve
me no more."

26. THE COMPASS

THE TRIAL WORE ON. THE COURT HAD PRACTICALLY finished with the witnesses now. The woodsmen, the police, the local magistrate, the sergeant, had all testified. The baker N, too, and his wife Elizabeth, had told us all they knew. It amounted to nothing.

The baker hadn't been able to resist mentioning the opinion I had voiced about the negroes. He threw out dark hints against my seditious beliefs, while the President watched him doubtfully—though not daring to interrupt him.

Z's mother was the next to be called. She left her place and went into the box. The President explained to her that she was entitled, if she chose, to decline to testify. But she wished to.

She had removed her veil.

Z was a quiet, but at times a violently tempered child, she told the court, in her rather unpleasant voice—and it was from his father that he had inherited his temper. He had had no illnesses—apart from the harmless ailments that children usually go through. Nor was there any trace of mental disease in the family, either on his father's side or hers.

"Your honour," she interrupted suddenly. "May I ask my son a question?"

"Certainly."

She went over to the table, took the compass, and turned to Z.

"How long have you had a compass?" she asked, and her voice trembled with scorn. "You've never had one. We had an argument about it before you went to camp, because you were saying everybody had one. 'I'm the only one without a compass,' you said, 'and I shall get lost without one.' So how did you come by this one?"

Z stared at her.

She turned to the President in triumph.

"It isn't his compass. Whoever lost this compass is responsible for the crime."

A murmur went through the court-room.

"Do you hear what your mother says?" the President asked Z.

The boy was still staring at her.

"Yes," came the slow answer. "My mother's lying."

The defending counsel sprang up.

"I propose the appointment of a commission to examine the accused's mental condition."

The President reassured him that the court would take up the question later.

Z's mother returned to the boy's side.

"I'm lying? You said—?"

"Yes."

"I'm not lying. I've never in my life told a lie, but you've always lied, always. I'm telling the truth, and only the truth, but you still want to shield this strumpet, this prostitute—"

"She's not—"

"Hold your tongue," shrieked the mother, hysterical by

now. "You think of nothing but that poisonous wretch, you never think of your mother, your poor mother."

"The girl's worth more than you are!"

"Quiet!" cried the President, condemning Z to two days for insulting a witness.

"Unprecedented!" he deplored. "The way you treat your mother! It reveals a lot."

Z lost control of himself, and the temper that he had inherited from his father broke out.

"She isn't a mother! She isn't. She's never bothered about me, only about her servants. Ever since I've been born, I've heard her hateful voice nagging at the maids in the kitchen."

"He always takes the girls' side, like my husband, your honour." She laughed shortly.

"Don't laugh!" roared Z. "Do you remember Thekla?"

"And what of Thekla?"

"She was fifteen, and you wore her down as nobody else could. She had to go on ironing till eleven at night and be up in the morning at half-past four—and nothing to eat, either. And she ran away. Do you remember?"

"Yes, she used to steal!"

"So that she could get out of it all. I was six then, I can still remember Dad coming home and telling me that the poor girl had been caught. She was sent to a reformatory. And it was your fault, only yours."

"Mine?"

"My father said so."

"Your father said a great many things."

"But he never lied. You used to have terrible quarrels and he wouldn't sleep at home. Do you remember? And

Eve's another one like Thekla—near enough. No, mother, I've no love for you now."

When the outburst had finished, it was very quiet in the court-room.

"Thank you, madam," said the President.

27. THE BOX

MY TURN NOW.

It was already a quarter to five.

I was sworn as a witness. I swore by God to tell the truth to the best of my ability, and to conceal nothing.

Nothing.

I noticed a certain tension in the room.

I turned round and caught sight of Eve.

She was sitting beside the wardress. Once, I had wanted to see her eyes. When I've told them everything, I thought, I'll look. I can't now. I must turn my back to her, for before me I saw a crucifix: His Son.

I glanced at Z.

He was smiling. Was she too smiling, behind my back?

I answered the President's questions. He touched upon the negroes again—yes, we understood each other. I gave good characters to N and to Z too. The President was discharging me from the witness-box when I interrupted him.

"One moment, your honour—if I may."

"Please."

"That box, in which Z kept his diary. It wasn't N who broke it open."

"Not N? Who was it, then?"

"Myself. I opened the box with a piece of wire."

My words produced an immense effect. The President

dropped his pencil, counsel jumped up, Z stared at me open-mouthed, while his mother screamed and the baker's hand flew to his heart, his face as pale as dough.

And Eve?

I don't know what she did.

I was aware only of a general uneasiness behind me. Amid murmurs and whispers, the public prosecutor rose as if hypnotized, slowly raising his finger in my direction.

"You?"

The word took him a long moment to pronounce.

"Yes," I answered, amazed at my own calm, and inexpressibly relieved. I told the court everything now—why I had broken open the box and why I hadn't admitted as much to Z immediately. I told them I had been ashamed to—and not only ashamed, but too much of a coward in the bargain. I told them why I'd read the diary and why I had not informed the police about the theft—because I wanted to frustrate those plans, if I could.

Now I noticed that the prosecutor was beginning to take my words down, but I went on, unhindered. I omitted nothing. Adam and Eve, the dark clouds, the man in the moon, all—and when I'd come to a close, the prosecutor stood up.

"I should like to impress upon the witness that he must be fully aware of the grave consequences of his interesting testimony. The prosecution retains the right to accuse him of misleading the authorities, and of being an accessory to theft."

I made him a slight bow.

"I swore to conceal nothing," I said.

And the baker roared out:

"My son's death lies at his door—his only!"

A sudden heart attack necessitated his being helped from the court-room. His wife raised a threatening arm.

"Beware of God!" she cried to me. "Beware of God!"

But I had no fear now of God.

I recognized the aversion, the loathing, around me. All eyes were charged with it—save two that rested on me, two eyes as still as the dark pools in the little woods of my homeland.

Eve . . .

28. EXPELLED FROM PARADISE

"Do you know what this is?" asked the President, holding out the compass.

"Yes," she answered. "That shows the direction."

"Do you know to whom it belongs?"

"It's not mine."

"Don't lie."

"I'm not lying. I'd like to tell the truth like the teacher did."

Like me? The public prosecutor smiled ironically. The counsel for the defence watched Eve every second.

"Go on, then," ordered the President.

"When I found Z near our caves, N came along too."

"You were there?"

"Yes."

"Why do you only tell us that now? Why did you keep lying throughout the examination? You said you weren't present when Z struck N."

"He didn't strike N."

"He didn't? Who did?"

The tension grew even greater. Every one in the room leaned forward, as if they would drive her into the earth.

Z's face was chalk white.

"Z and N were having a terrible struggle. N was stronger. He threw Z down off the rock. I thought, He's done for now, and I got mad, and then it struck me he'd seen the diary and knew everything about me. I picked up a stone, that one there, and started after him. I wanted to get him on the head—yes, I wanted to right enough, but suddenly another boy, I didn't know him, sprang out of the bushes. He took the stone off me and went on running after N. I saw him catch up and speak to him. They were just by a clear bit. He'd got the stone in his hand all the time. I hid. I was afraid they'd both be coming back. But they didn't come back, they went off another way, N a couple of steps in front. Suddenly this other boy lifted up the stone and caught N on the head with it from behind. N fell down and didn't move again. The other boy bent over him close, then he dragged him away. Into a ditch. He didn't know I'd been watching. I ran back to the rock and found Z there. The crash hadn't hurt him, his coat was a bit torn and his hands were scratched."

The defending counsel was the first to recover his speech.

"I propose that the charge against Z be dismissed."

"One moment, Doctor," the President broke in, turning to Z, who was still staring at the girl like a ghost. "Do we know that she is telling the truth?"

"She is," murmured Z.

"Then did you too see this other boy striking N?"

"No, I didn't see it."

"Well!" The public prosecutor breathed again and leant back reassured.

"So it was you who struck him?" observed the defence.

The girl spoke quite calmly.

"It wasn't me."

"We'll come back to that," said the President. "I'd like to

hear now why you've concealed this until to-day, if you're not guilty. Well?"

Both Z and the girl were silent for a moment. Then it was she, again, who spoke.

"Z took it on himself, because he thought it was me that'd killed N. He couldn't believe it was somebody else."

"And are we to believe that?"

She smiled again.

"I don't know. That's how it was, though."

"And would you have sat quietly by and seen Z sent to prison?"

"Not quietly, sir. I've done enough crying. But I was so afraid of the reformatory again—and now I've told you he's not guilty."

"Why only now?"

"Because the teacher told the truth as well, I think."

"Remarkable!" from the prosecutor.

"And what if the teacher hadn't?" inquired the President.

"I thought," came a sarcastic observation from the defending counsel, "I thought you loved Z. That's very different from real love!"

There was a smile at this.

Eve faced the lawyer who had evoked it.

"No," she said quietly. "I don't love him."

Z jumped up.

"I've never loved him," she said, her voice a little stronger. Then she lowered her head. Z sat down again slowly, and looked at his right hand. He wanted to shield her, but she didn't love him. He wanted to go to prison for her . . .

What was Z thinking of now? Of his forfeited career—as an inventor, or a mail pilot? Everything had happened amiss. Soon he would hate Eve.

29. THE FISH

"NOW," CONTINUED THE PRESIDENT, AS THE examination of Eve proceeded. "You admit to having followed N with this stone?"

"Yes, sir."

"And you wanted to kill him?"

"But I didn't."

"What did you do instead?"

"I've already said. A boy I hadn't seen before came up, knocked me down, and went off after N with the stone."

"Can you describe this boy in any way?"

"He went so quick I couldn't—"

"Aha! The Mysterious Unknown!" interpolated the prosecutor.

"Would you recognize him again?" asked the President deprecatingly.

"Perhaps. I'm not sure—only I remember now he had bright round eyes, like a fish."

I sprang up and repeated the word.

"What—what is it?" I heard from the President.

Every one was equally astounded.

I asked myself—what?

I was thinking of that illuminated death's head. Cold times are coming—the Age of the Fish. The soul of man is hardening till it will be like the face of a fish. Two bright, round eyes stared at me. Unblinking, lustreless.

T's eyes.

I saw him standing at the open grave—and in the camp, too, with that same quiet, supercilious smile of scorn. Had he known all along that it was I who broke open the box? Had he too read the diary? and spied? and run after Z and N?

That strange, fixed smile.

I remained calm.

"What is it?" came the question, a second time.

Should I tell him that T was in my thoughts? Absurd. Why should T strike N dead? No motive.

"I'm sorry, your honour," I said. "My nerves are a little on edge."

"Understandable enough," grinned the President.

I left the court. I knew they would acquit Z and sentence the girl. But I knew too that in the end, everything would come right.

The next day, or the next, proceedings would be instituted against me. For withholding information, and for being an accessory to theft. My position as a teacher would be suspended. I'd lose my bread and butter. The thought didn't trouble me.

I might not have enough to eat.

It was comical how little anxiety I felt.

I thought of the bar where I could find Julius Caesar. It was cheap enough. But I didn't get drunk there. I went back to my room and lay down. The fear of my room had quite gone.

Was this His dwelling now?

30. THE FISH WON'T BITE

THERE IT WAS, IN THE MORNING PAPERS.

Z, convicted on a charge of being an accessory to theft, had, in view of mitigating circumstances, received only a short sentence. But the public prosecutor had instigated criminal proceedings against the girl, the charge being first-degree murder.

"The wanton creature obstinately maintained her innocence," wrote the crime reporter, "but it is doubtful whether anyone present was convinced in the slightest degree by her screams. It is a notorious fact that whoever lies once will lie again. Z, the accused, did not even go so far as to offer her his hand when towards the end of the proceedings she tore herself from the wardress and rushed over to him, imploring his forgiveness for having never loved him."

Ah, he hates her now, I thought. And now she is utterly alone—still crying? Don't cry now, Eve: I believe you. Wait, I'll hook the fish.

I didn't quite know how to go about it, but it seemed to me that the sooner I got in touch with him, the better.

The post that morning brought me a letter from the authorities to the effect that I must keep away from the high school until the proceedings against me had been satisfactorily concluded. I supposed I had seen the high school for the last time, since I obviously stood a scanty chance of acquittal; and in my case there were no mitigating circumstances. But all that meant nothing to me now: until I found him, I should constantly hear Eve's cries.

A little shyly, my landlady brought in my breakfast. She'd read my testimony in the paper, and the city echoed with my name. The reporters were busy. "TEACHER AIDS THEFT" ran one of the headlines—and in one paper I found myself accused of moral guilt for the crime. No one was on my side. A good day, this, for Mr. N, the masterbaker—provided the devil didn't come for him last night.

Midday found me near the school. I dared no longer enter, waiting for the morning lessons to finish. It seemed ages before the boys came out. Some of my colleagues were among them. They looked away. And here was T, by himself. As I slowly crossed the road in his direction, he caught sight of me and hung on his step. For a moment—then he greeted me with a smile.

"I'm so glad I've run into you," I said. "I've got several things we can talk over."

"By all means, sir."

He nodded politely.

"There's not enough quiet out here in the street—can I invite you to have an ice with me somewhere?"

"Thank you, sir."

We took our places in a café, where my companion ordered a lemon and strawberry ice. Even as he was eating it, the smile seemed to remain on his face. And suddenly I began.

"I wanted to have a word with you over the trial."

Unperturbed, he dug his spoon into his ice-cream.

"D'you like it?" I murmured.

"Yes."

We paused.

"Tell me," I went on, "do you think it was the girl who murdered N?"

"Yes, sir."

"So you don't think that another boy could have done it?"

"No. She only invented that to wriggle out of it."

And we paused again—until he put down his spoon for a moment and looked up at me doubtfully.

"What do you really want of me, sir?"

I spoke slowly, into those round eyes.

"I thought you might have an idea as to who the boy was."

"Me? Why?"

I risked it.

"Because I know that you're always spying," I said.

"Yes," he replied quietly. "I have observed—various things."

He smiled again. Had he known all along about the box?

"Have you read the diary?" I asked.

He met my eyes.

"No. But I watched you, sir, when you slipped out of the camp and eavesdropped on Z and the girl."

I felt very cold under his stare.

"You touched my face. I was standing behind you. You were terribly frightened, but I wasn't at all."

He took up his spoon again.

And suddenly it occurred to me that he wasn't relishing my confusion. From time to time he threw me a thoughtful glance, as if he wanted to learn something from me.

Curious—I thought of a hunter watching with infinite patience, and then, when certain of his mark, pulling the trigger. A hunter who found no thrill in his sport.

But why should T turn hunter?

"Were you on good terms with N?" I asked.

"Yes. Very good terms."

How dearly I should have liked to ask him why he had struck N and killed him!

"You're speaking to me, sir," he told me suddenly, "as if I were the other boy—as if I'd killed N. Although you're aware that no one knows what the other boy looks like—if he exists at all. Even the girl can only say he had eyes like a fish—and I haven't. They're more like the eyes of a doe, my mother and everybody says so. Why do you smile, sir? I should say that rather than me, it's you who've got eyes like a fish—"

"Me?"

"Don't you know, then, sir, the nickname you've got in school? Haven't you ever heard it? It's 'the fish.'"

He nodded as he smiled.

"Yes, really, sir—because you always have such an expressionless face. One never knows what you're thinking—or whether you really trouble about anyone. We always say the teacher just looks on, a man could be run over in the street, and he'd just watch him lying there and he wouldn't do a thing, even if the other fellow were dying—"

He came to a sudden stop, as if he'd said too much, and for a fraction of a second there was fear in his eyes as he glanced at me.

Why fear?

Ah, you almost had the hook in your mouth, but you didn't bite, for you saw the line, and you swam down into your depths again. But if you aren't hooked, you've given yourself away and I'll catch you yet . . .

He got up.

"I must go home now, sir, my lunch will be waiting. If I'm late, I'll get into a row."

With a word of thanks for the ice, he left me. I watched him out of sight, and could hear the girl crying.

31. A FLAG DAY

ON WAKING NEXT MORNING, I SEEMED TO emerge from a mist of amorphous and forgotten dreams.

The Greatest Plebeian's birthday meant a holiday today, and the town was decked out with flags and streamers. Through the streets marched the young girls who had searched for the lost airman, the boys who would have left the negroes to die, and their parents, who believed the lies inscribed upon their banners. Even the sceptical joined in the march and kept time with the rest—spineless divisions under an idiot's command. As they marched, they sang—of a bird fluttering upon a hero's grave, of a soldier suffocating in the fumes of poison gas, of brown girls and black girls who lived on filth, of an enemy that only existed in their minds. With their songs, the liars and the debased celebrated the day on which the Great Plebeian had been born.

From my window too, a flag was waving. I noticed it with a certain gratification: I had hung it out the night before. For if you are ruled by the lawless and the debased you had better adopt their methods or they might flay you alive. You must drape your home with flags—even if you've a home no longer. When submissiveness is the solitary trait in the human character that those who rule will tolerate, truth flies away and lies creep in—the lies that engender sin. But don't wait—hang out the flags. Better bread than death.

But had I forgotten that my own position in the high school had been suspended? I committed no perjury, I told them the truth about the box. I could hang out my flags, grovel in the dust before that filth and tell what lies I liked—it wouldn't alter the fact that my bread was lost!

Don't forget, I whispered to myself, that you've come to know a higher authority than those who reign out there. Your house, your room, isn't quite the one you've known. It's part of another dwelling now and within it the very furniture has changed.

Look out of the window, see how far beneath you that procession looks now, how diminished. And those rich plebeians—how poor they look! And those flags, how faded and bedraggled. The message inscribed on those banners is too far away for you to read, the radio drones too faintly, and Eve's lightest sob can quell it. But her sobs have died, too, into hushed tears . . .

Her tears were all I heard.

32. ONE OF THE FIVE

I WAS JUST CLEANING MY TEETH WHEN MY landlady knocked.

"There's one of the high school boys outside," she said. "He'd like to see you."

"Just a moment."

She left me. I put on my dressing-gown. It had been a Christmas present from my parents.

"You can't live without a dressing-gown," they said—so they'd given me this one: green and mauve, for they've no taste.

There was a knock at the door. Which of the boys could it be? T?

"Come in," I said.

He entered with a little bow. I didn't recognize him for a second. It was B. Of the five B's in my form, this was the one I had noticed least. What did he want with me? How was it that he wasn't out there, marching with the others?

"Sir," he began, "I've been wondering for a long time whether it was worth telling you or not—and now I've decided to."

"Yes?"

"The mystery over the compass—I've had no peace of mind—"

"The compass?"

"Yes, sir. I read in the papers that by the side of N they found a compass, and nobody knows who it belongs to."

"Well—?"

"I know who lost it, sir."

"Who?"

"T."

T swimming up out of his depths once more? Showing his head above the dark surface—?

"How do you happen to know this compass belonged to him?" I asked my young visitor, trying to put on a show of indifference.

"He was looking for it everywhere—we had the same tent, sir."

In the silence that followed, he averted his eyes. Then:

"Do you believe that T could have done it?" I said.

He stared at me; then:

"I'd believe anything of anybody, sir."

"But not murder?"

"Why not?"

And he smiled. But not with scorn: with sadness.

"But why should T have killed N? Where's the motive?"

"T was always saying that N was a fool."

"Well, there's not much ground there—"

"No, sir. But you know T is horribly inquisitive, he always wants to know—how things really are—and he told me once, he would like to see someone die."

"What!"

"Yes, he would like to see the reality of it. And he's always imagining what birth would be like: he's said he would like to see a child coming into the world."

Speechless for the moment, I went over to the window. The children and their parents were still marching by—and it struck me suddenly—why was B here?

"Why aren't you out marching with the others?" I asked him. "It's your duty."

"I said I didn't feel well." He grinned.

An understanding glance passed between us.

"I won't give you away," I reassured him.

"I know!"

How much do you know of me? I thought.

"I don't want to do any more marching, and I can't stand being ordered about—with fellows yelling at you just because they're a year or two older. And those eternal speeches, the same trashy rubbish that we're sick and tired of."

I had to smile.

"It's to be hoped that you're the only boy in the form that thinks so."

"Oh, no, there's four of us already."

Already?

"Do you remember, sir, when you said that about the niggers—last Easter term, before the camp? We all signed that letter that we didn't want you to teach us any more. But I only did it under compulsion—of course you were right about the negroes! And one by one, I got hold of three others who thought so too."

"Who are they?"

"I can't tell you, sir. Our rules won't let me."

"Your rules?"

"Yes, sir. We've founded a club. We've got two more now, but they're not schoolboys. One's a baker's apprentice and the other's an errand boy."

"A club?"

"We meet once a week and read everything that's forbidden."

"Aha!"

What was it that Julius Caesar had said? "They read

everything in secret, but only to pour their scorn on it. Scorn is their ideal. Cold times are coming."

I put it to B.

"And so you sit there in your club pouring your scorn on everything, I suppose?"

"Oh, no! Scorn is absolutely forbidden—that's in rule three. There are some, I know, who've only got contempt for everything—T's like that, for one, but we haven't. We meet and talk over everything we've read."

"What then?"

"Then we go on to discuss how things should be in the world."

I pricked up my ears. How things should be! I heard Z's words again, to the President: "Our teacher is always telling us how things should be in the world and never how they really are!"

With my mind's eye, I saw T's face too. What had Eve said? "N fell down. The other boy bent over him and watched him. Then he dragged him into the ditch."

And what had B said just now? "T always wanted to know how things really are." Why did he want to know? So that he could make everything the object of his contempt? Yes, cold times were coming.

B was speaking again.

"One can tell you everything, sir. That's why I came along to you, to tell you of my suspicions, to talk it over with you and consider what we ought to do."

"Why did you come to me?"

"In the club, yesterday, when we read about your confession and the broken box—we all said you were the only grown-up person we knew who had any love for the truth."

33. THE CLUB STEPS IN

TO-DAY I WENT ALONG TO THE MAGISTRATE with B. Yesterday, his office was naturally closed on account of the festivities.

I informed him that quite possibly B knew to whom the compass belonged. But he waved my explanation politely aside and told me that the question of the compass had now been settled. It had been established beyond all doubt that the instrument had been stolen from the mayor of the little town which lay near the camp. Presumably the girl had dropped it, or if not the girl, then at any rate one of the boys of her gang—and perhaps on an earlier occasion when he was passing the same spot; for the crime had taken place close to their home, the caves. The compass was out of it now.

B did not conceal his disappointment as we left.

But was the compass really out of it? Hadn't it proved the reason for B's visit to my rooms yesterday?

Perhaps I had changed my way of thinking: I was waiting for connecting links now. For the slightest thing could play its part; and I was aware of strange forces at work . . .

On the steps of the building, we bumped into the defending counsel. He greeted me warmly.

"I wanted to write and thank you," he told me. "It was only your fearless and unselfish statement that made it possible for me to clear up this tragic affair."

He informed me in a word or two that Z had been completely cured of his infatuation, and that the girl was suffering from attacks of hysteria, and was now lying in the prison hospital. "Poor devil," he muttered as he hurried off, perhaps to clear up more tragedies. As I watched him disappear round the corner, I heard B's voice:

"I'm sorry for that girl."

"I too," I answered.

We went down onto the street.

"We ought to see what we can do," he went on.

"Yes."

I was thinking of her eyes—and of those still pools in the little woods of my homeland. Still the clouds passed over the prison hospital where she lay—the silver-hemmed clouds. I tried to remember whether or not she had nodded to me, in the court-room, before she came out with the truth. But T had said she was only trying to lie her way out.

I hated T.

I stopped short suddenly.

"Tell me, B—is it true that I've got a nickname in my form—'the fish'?"

"Why, no! That's what T said. You've got a different one altogether."

"What is it?"

"We call you 'the Nigger.'"

We laughed.

We had reached the pavement now.

"Sir," said B, grave once again. "Don't you think it could have been T, even if the compass didn't belong to him?"

What should I answer to that? What ought I to answer— "Perhaps"? "Possibly"? "Under the circumstances"—?

"Yes," I said. "I think he's the culprit."

B's eyes lit up.

"He was! And we'll catch him!"

"Let us hope so."

"I'll put a motion through in the club, that we've got to help that girl. Paragraph seven says we don't just meet to read books, but to live by them."

"What's your motto?"

"Justice—and truth."

He was quite worked up. The club would keep track of T's every movement, day and night, and report to me daily.

"Fine," I said, though with an involuntary smile. We used to play Indians too, when I was a boy. Our happy hunting-ground was an imaginary one.

But to-day it is real.

34. TWO LETTERS

NEXT MORNING I RECEIVED A VERY UPSETTING letter from my people. They were beside themselves with grief because I'd lost my job. Hadn't I given them a thought when I'd made that entirely unnecessary confession about the box? Why on earth did I have to make it?

But I hadn't forgotten them: and I knew we needn't worry; we shouldn't starve.

"We couldn't sleep the whole night," my mother wrote, "for thinking of you."

And my father—"What have we done to deserve this?"

My father is a retired foreman, and he has his pension.

I thought of God: He still might not dwell with them, although they went to church every Sunday.

I sat down to answer their letter.

"My dear parents," I began, "You mustn't worry, God will see us through . . ."

But for some reason or another, I couldn't go on. They knew I had never believed in God. "Things are going against him now," they'd think, "so he remembers Him again." I didn't want anyone to think that. It would shame me. I tore up my letter, for I was proud still. During the rest of the day, I was determined to write to my parents, but I couldn't do it. I couldn't get beyond the first line or two, and write down the word "God."

When evening came, I felt sudden fears of my room again. It was so empty. I went out, with the vague intention of going to the cinema, but instead I found myself in the little bar—with Julius Caesar, its figure-head. He beamed when he saw me.

"Wonderful of you to speak up about that affair of the broken lock. I'd never have done it. The most admirable thing for ages."

We talked about the trial over a drink. He was all ears when I told him about the fish.

"Of course it must be T," he agreed. He smiled. "If I can be of any use to you in catching him, I am at your service, for I too, my friend—I too have my connections—"

Our little talk was interrupted from time to time, for others would come up to Julius Caesar, with the same object as myself. They valued his advice, for they knew him for a wise and understanding fellow. He was hail-fellow-well-met with them all.

Despair seized me. What were we all but weeds?

Avi, Caesar, morituri te salutamus.

I felt a sudden yearning for the decadence I saw at my side. How I'd like to have worn an illuminated death's head in my tie!

"Be careful—you've dropped a letter out of your pocket," said my friend.

"Ah, yes! My letter."

Caesar went on to explain to a young woman the new paragraph in the morality code.

I thought of Eve. What would Eve be like in a few more years, when she was as old as Caesar's companion? Who could help her?

I moved over to another table and wrote to my parents.

"You must not worry. God will help us."

And this time, I didn't tear the letter up.

Perhaps I'd only written it because of the drinks I'd had. What did it matter, anyway?

35. AUTUMN

NEXT DAY MY LANDLADY HANDED ME AN envelope which, apparently, an errand boy had brought. A blue envelope which I opened with a smile.

I read the heading:

"First Report of the Club."

Beneath it:

"Nothing special to report."

Ha! The good old club, fighting for justice and truth—and yet it can't find anything special to report. Nor can I.

What could be done to save Eve? She was still in my thoughts, and to such an extent that I wondered if I loved the girl I wanted to help. I'd had many women, I was no saint. And women aren't saints. But this was a different feeling. Did it mean that my youth had passed and given place to age?

I shouldn't have had those fears, for it was still summer. But every day I went on receiving that blue envelope—and nothing special to report inside.

The days went by. The apples were ripe now, and mists stole over the evenings. Cattle were driven home again, their summer pastures were barren. It was summer still, yet already one thought of winter's snow.

I wanted to help her against the cold too. I should have liked to buy her a coat and shoes and underwear: I wouldn't have expected anything in return.

Could the snow come yet?

Everything was still green.

But I couldn't be at her side.

If only I knew that everything would go well with her!

36. A VISITOR

THIS MORNING I HAD A VISITOR.

I didn't recognize him at once. It was the priest with whom I had once talked about human ideals. He was in mufti—dark grey trousers and a bluish coat. I was surprised. Had he left the Church?

"You may well wonder at my clothes." He smiled. "But I'm generally in mufti now. I'm in rather a curious position. To put it shortly, my period of punishment is over. Anyway, we'll leave me out of it, and talk about you. I read about your courageous testimony in the papers. I should have turned up before, but I had to get hold of your address first. You strike me as having changed quite noticeably. I don't know exactly how to describe it, but something about you is different. Yes, you seem much more cheerful!"

"More cheerful?"

"Yes. So you should be, after speaking up about the broken box, even if the world does malign you. I've often thought of you, although you once told me that you didn't believe in God—or perhaps that was the reason. Meanwhile, perhaps you've started to have a rather different idea of God . . ."

I looked at him mistrustfully. What did he want with me?

"I've something of importance to tell you, but first of

all, will you be so good as to answer two questions? In the first place, I suppose you're wide awake to the fact that even if the case against you should be dropped, you will never be allowed to teach again in any high school in the country?"

"Yes, I was well aware of that before I made my statement."

"I'm very glad. And now—how do you propose to live? I take it you aren't one of the shareholders in the saw-mills, since on one occasion you spoke so fervently for the piece-workers and the children in the windows—do you remember?"

Yes! The children in the windows. I'd forgotten them. And the saw-mill that lay idle. How far away it all seemed now, like part of another life!

"I've nothing," I said. "And I have to support my parents."

"I've got something for you," he said, after a short pause.

"What? A job?"

"Yes, but abroad."

"Where?"

"In Africa."

"With the negroes?"

I smiled—I, "the Nigger."

The priest did not smile.

"What do you find so comical in that? Negroes are men too."

You needn't have told me that, I smiled to myself. But I didn't say anything, and listened to his proposal. I could become a teacher in a mission school.

"Should I have to take orders?" I asked.

"Not necessarily."

I was thoughtful for a moment. Now I believed in God,

but I didn't believe that white men brought any blessing to black: they brought God, but only as a part and parcel of a thousand dubious gifts. I told the priest so. His calm remained.

"It depends upon you entirely, whether you misuse your mission or not."

"My mission?"

"Yes, every one has a mission," he said.

Right! But I had to find the truth in those round bright eyes of T. I must catch the fish first.

I told the priest I'd go to Africa, but only when I'd succeeded in freeing the girl. He listened closely. Then he gave me this advice:

"If you really think that this other boy did it, then you must tell his mother. A mother must hear everything. Go to her straight away."

37. THE TERMINUS

I WAS ON MY WAY TO T'S MOTHER.

The school secretary had given me the address—but very reluctantly, for I was supposed to keep away from the high school. I had passed its threshold for the last time: soon I should be in Africa.

My tram rattled on through streets of smart houses, which slowly gave way before ugliness and poverty. Beyond, lay the villas of the rich.

"Terminus!" shouted the conductor. "Terminus. All change."

I was his only fare.

The air was much fresher here than in my own neighbourhood. The gardens were well kept, and here there were no garden dwarfs, no reclining fawns, no mushrooms.

At last I found the number I wanted—thirty-one. The gate was high and the house hidden in its grounds.

My ring brought out an old porter, but he did not immediately open up.

"Yes, sir?"

"I'd like to see Mrs. T."

"On what business?"

"I'm her son's teacher."

"Certainly."

He opened the gate and we walked up the drive. As we

passed a black fir-tree, I caught sight of the house. A palace, almost. A servant was waiting, and I was handed over to his charge.

"The gentleman would like to see the lady. He's the young gentleman's teacher."

The footman nodded.

"That might be difficult, sir," he said politely. "We have visitors just now."

"I'm afraid it's extremely important," I said.

"Could you arrange to come to-morrow?"

"No. It's about her son."

He smiled, with a slight, negative gesture.

"Even so—my mistress often hasn't got time for her son. Even the young gentleman himself generally has to send in his name first."

"Look here," I said with a dangerous look, "send in mine now, or you'll answer for the consequences."

He stared at me quite whitely for a second, and then bowed.

"Well, we'll try! Excuse me if I lead the way."

I went in. Through a splendid hall and up the staircase. We encountered a woman who as she went downstairs smiled at the footman and me.

"That was the film-star X," whispered the footman.

Of course, I'd seen her quite recently—as a little factory girl who married the boss. She was a friend of the Chief Plebeian. Poetry and Justice! I thought.

"She's a divine artist," murmured the footman as we reached the first floor. Through an open door, I heard women laughing—from the third room, I thought. And then the chink of tea-cups. The footman took me into a little drawing-room and asked me if I would please wait, he would do all he could, and take the first opportunity on my behalf. He closed the door as he left me.

It was afternoon, and by no means late, but the days were growing shorter.

I looked at some old prints on the walls. Jupiter-Jove, Amor, Psyche. Marie Antoinette. The room was rose and gold. How old were those chairs that stood around the table? Nearly two hundred years, perhaps. Those who'd sat in them might have gone to the execution of Marie Antoinette.

Where was Eve now? Still in the prison hospital, I hoped. There at least she'd have a bed.

Unless she'd got well again!

I went over to the window and looked out.

The fir-tree shadow stood blacker in the twilight.

At last the door slowly opened. I turned round: now I should see T's mother. But it wasn't T's mother who stood there. It was the boy himself.

"My mother sent me to you," he said courteously, "when she heard you were here, sir. She's sorry she has no time—"

"Oh? When will she have time?"

He shrugged his shoulders wearily.

"I don't know. She never has time."

Never has time. What has she to do, then? She must think of no one but herself. My thoughts went back to the priest, and our conversation about human ideals. Was it true that victory always lay with the rich? Could not the wine turn to water?

"If your mother's always occupied," I said, "perhaps I could see your father?"

"My father? But he's never at home. I scarcely ever see him. He's got his business."

His business?

I thought of the saw-mill that sawed no longer, and the children sitting in the windows painting dolls. They were saving light: they had no light.

God goes through every street. God sees the children and the saw-mill. God might have come here, to be faced by the old porter and the same questions at that high gate. The porter would inquire why He wanted to see T's parents. Perhaps they knew: but they never expected Him.

"Why do you wish to see my parents, sir?"

I looked at T as he spoke, and waited for his smile to return. But T did not smile. He only stared. There was a shimmer of sudden terror in his eyes.

"I wanted to have a word with your parents about you," I said, "but unfortunately they've no time."

"About me?"

He grinned.

An empty grin.

The boy who had wanted to steal the secrets of life and death stood there like an idiot— and as if he were listening to something.

What could he hear?

The creaking flight of madness?

I hurried away.

38. THE BAIT

AT HOME ANOTHER BLUE ENVELOPE AWAITED ME.
Nothing special to report again?
I opened it and read:

EIGHTH REPORT OF THE CLUB
Yesterday afternoon T went to the Crystal Cinema.
When he left, he was talking to an elegant lady whom
he must have met inside. He then accompanied her
to 67 Y-Street. Half an hour later he appeared again
with her at the door, and left her. He went home.
The lady watched him, made a face and deliberately
spat after him. It is possible that she was no lady. She
was tall and a blonde, wore a dark green coat and a
red hat. Otherwise, nothing special to report.

I grinned. T was getting gay. But it wasn't that which
interested me. Why should she have made a face at him? Of
course she was no lady! But why did she spit?

I'd go and ask her. For now I was determined to follow
up the slightest, silliest incident.

If he wasn't to be hooked, we'd catch him in a net, a fine-
meshed net that he couldn't slip through.

I went to 67 Y-Street and asked the woman who came
to the door if I might see a blond lady—

"Miss Nelly has room seventeen," she interjected.

The other people in the house were honest folk of the lower middle-class.

I rang at door number seventeen.

It was opened by a blonde.

"Hallo! Come in!" she said.

I'd never seen her before.

In the room I could see the dark green coat hanging up, and the red hat lying on the table. This was the woman. She was angry when she found that I'd only come for information. When I promised to pay her for it, her resentment gave way to distrust. No, I wasn't the police, I told her, in an attempt to remove it. I only wanted to know why she'd spat after that boy yesterday.

"Let's see the money," she said.

I gave it to her. She made herself comfortable on the sofa and offered me a cigarette. We smoked.

"I don't want to rake it up again," she said, and then paused.

Suddenly she came out with it.

"I'll soon tell you why I spat at him. It made me sick, I couldn't stand him."

She shuddered.

"How d'you mean?"

"How would you like it? He was laughing!"

"Laughing?"

"It gave me the creeps. And then I got so wild I boxed his ears. He ran across to the mirror. 'It isn't red!' he says. He was just watching all the time, to see what it was like. If I had my way, I wouldn't touch that fellow with a bargepole, but I'm sorry to say I shall have the pleasure once more—"

"Are you forced to, then?"

"You don't force Nelly to nothing. I'm just doing some-body a favour of my own sweet will in going with that lousy cur again—I've got to act as if I was in love with him this time—"

"You're doing somebody a favour?"

"Yeah. It's somebody I owe a lot to."

"Who?"

"Oh, you don't get no more change out of me. Some-body you wouldn't know."

"What's he want, then, this somebody?"

She fixed her eyes on mine, and drawled:

"He wants to catch a fish!"

I sprang up at the word.

She went white.

"What's up?" she gasped, stubbing out her cigarette. "That's all the talking I'm going to do to you. Looks like you're crazy. You get out of here. Good-bye."

I staggered out, my brain whirling with questions. Who'll catch the fish? What's happened now? Who's this stranger that's mixed up in it?

39. THE NET

I WENT BACK TO MY LODGINGS. MY LANDLADY met me with a worried look.

"There's a gentleman here I don't know. He's been waiting half an hour for you. There's something strange about him that gave me quite a turn. He's in the drawing-room."

I went in. My visitor was sitting in the dark, for it was evening now. I switched on the light.

Julius Caesar!

He and his death's head greeted me.

"Now prick up your ears, colleague."

"What is it?"

"I've got the fish."

"You've got—?"

"Yes. He's been swimming nearer and nearer to the bait—and to-night he'll bite. Come on, we'll have to hurry. The line's baited and it's high time we were moving."

"What d'you mean?—the bait?"

"All in good time."

We started at once.

"Where are we going?" I asked.

"To 'The Lily.'"

"Where?"

"How shall I put it, child? 'The Lily' is just a low dive."

He had set a good pace. It began to rain.

"Good." He chuckled. "When it rains, they bite better."

"What have you got up your sleeve?"

"I'll tell you everything over a drink. Come on, we're getting wet."

"But how does it happen that you're catching the fish without saying a word to me?"

"I wanted to surprise you. Leave me that pleasure, please."

Suddenly he halted—in spite of his haste and the fact that it was pouring by now. He gave me a long look, and spoke slowly, seeming to emphasize every word.

"You ask me why I'm catching the fish? You told me about him a day or two ago—d'you remember? Then you moved off to another table, and suddenly it struck me how wretched you were over that girl, and I felt I had to help you. Do you remember sitting down at that table—I think you wrote a letter?"

Yes, the letter to my parents. The letter in which I at last managed to write that phrase about God.

I tottered.

"What's the matter?" I heard Caesar say. "You've gone dead white."

"Nothing. It's nothing."

"It's high time you put a schnapps down."

Perhaps he was right. I was shivering. For one tiny moment I saw the net.

40. N

"THE LILY" WAS VERY HARD TO FIND, SO DARK was the whole neighbourhood. And inside, it was little brighter. But at least it was warmer, and there was no rain.

"The ladies are here already," said the hostess, indicating the third box.

"Bravo," smiled Caesar. He turned to me. "The ladies are my bait. Lob-worms!"

In the third box sat Nelly with a buxom girl who might have been a waitress. Nelly recognized me at once, but habit kept her greeting silent. She just smiled wryly.

Caesar frowned, puzzled.

"Where's the fish?" he asked quickly.

"Ain't shown up," droned Nelly's companion in a dreary monotone of a voice.

"I'm sitting waiting for him," said Nelly with a gracious smile.

"She waited two hours for him in front of the cinema."

"Two and a half"—and the smile dropped suddenly from Nelly's face. "I'm jolly glad that slime didn't turn up."

Caesar introduced me to the two women.

"Here, meet a former colleague of mine."

Nelly looked up at the ceiling, while her comrade eyed me critically. She straightened her brassière.

We sat down. The schnapps warmed me to the heart. We were the only party in "The Lily." The proprietress put on her glasses and started reading the newspaper. She leant over the bar and gave you the impression that she wanted to cover her ears with her hands. She hadn't an inkling as to what was going on, and it was a matter of indifference to her.

I wondered what Caesar had meant when he called these two women the bait—the lob-worms.

"Well, what's the plan?" I asked him.

He bent very close to me.

"My original idea was to keep you out of this, my dear colleague, for it's a pretty mess, and I didn't want you implicated. But then it occurred to me that it couldn't do any harm if we had another witness. The three of us, the two ladies and myself, wanted to reconstruct the crime."

"Reconstruct the crime?"

"After a fashion, yes."

"How d'you mean?"

"We want the fish to give us a repetition of the murder."

"What?"

"Yes. According to an old-fashioned and very ingenious plan, I wanted to reconstruct the whole affair in a bed."

"In a bed?"

"Note well, colleague"—he nodded and lit up his death's head. "Miss Nelly was to wait for the fish outside the cinema. He thinks she loves him."

He laughed. But Miss Nelly didn't join in. She made a face, and spat.

"Don't do that here," grinned her comrade. "Spitting forbidden by the authorities."

"The authorities can go to hell."

"Now, now, no politics," Caesar broke in, and turned to me again.

"Our plan was to get the fish drunk here in this box, till he couldn't go on swimming. Then we could have caught him in our hands. Then the two ladies would have taken him through that unobtrusive little door into their room: and then the logical sequence of events would be this—"

The fish, Julius Caesar went on to explain, would drop off to sleep, while Nelly lay on the floor, her comrade having covered her with a sheet and made her look like a corpse.

Then the buxom little girl was to rush in and shriek at the sleeping fish: "What have you done, lad, what have you done?"

Caesar himself would open the door at that moment, call for the police, and accuse the drunken fish of having murdered Nelly, as he'd murdered that other one.

"We'd have had a great scene, colleague. I'd have given him a box on the ear into the bargain—I'll bet he'd have given himself away, if only by the merest word—and I'd have landed him by now."

I had to smile.

Caesar looked at me, perhaps indignantly. Then he went on:

"You're right. Man proposes and God disposes. While we sit here getting annoyed because somebody won't bite, all the time they may be floundering in the net."

The net . . .

Then I heard Caesar saying:

"You can't forget the girl who's innocent; but I'm thinking of the murdered boy, too."

The murdered boy? Yes, N. I'd totally forgotten him. I'd thought of everything else—I'd even thought of his parents, if not very graciously. But never for a moment of N himself.

N, murdered, struck down by a stone. N, who existed no more.

41. THE GHOST

I LEFT "THE LILY" AND TURNED HOMEWARDS; and now my thoughts of the dead N would give me no peace. They stayed with me even in my room, they were in my bed. I tried to force myself to sleep. It was useless.

I kept hearing N's voice.

"You've forgotten, sir, that you too share in the guilt of my murder. Who broke open the box? You or I? Didn't I appeal to you then, 'Help me, sir, I really didn't do it!'? But you wanted to frustrate those plans—I know, I know, it's over now."

Yes, finished.

Time may pass, but there are wounds that remain.

The minutes seemed to go faster and faster, passing me by. Soon the clock struck. I heard N's voice again.

"Do you remember a history lesson, sir, last winter term? We were doing the Middle Ages and you told us that the executioner, before the execution, would always ask the culprit's pardon for the wrong he was about to do him—for guilt can only be redeemed by guilt."

Was there no other way?

Am I the executioner? I wondered. Must I ask T's pardon? My thoughts overwhelmed me. I started up.

"Where are you going?"

"Away—far away."

"Stop."

N stood before me, barring my way. I could not get past him: I wanted his voice to cease.

He had no eyes now, and yet I could not escape his stare. I switched on the light, and noticed the lamp-shade. It was covered in dust.

And still I thought of T. Was he swimming up to the bait?

"Why do you think only of yourself?" asked N suddenly.

"Of myself?"

"You're still thinking of the fish. But you and the fish are one."

"One?"

"You want to catch him—don't you?"

"Yes—but how does that make him and me one?"

"You forget the executioner, sir—the hangman that must ask the murderer's pardon. In that secret hour when one sin is redeemed by another, the murderer and the executioner melt into one being—can you understand?"

Yes, gradually, I began to understand. But I wished to know no more.

Fear?

"Still you let him go on swimming," came N's voice. "Already you begin to pity him—"

Yes, his mother had no time . . .

"But you should think of my mother too, and, above all, of me. Even if you catch the fish, not for my sake, but for the sake of the girl—this girl who is in your thoughts no longer—"

He was right, I realized. It was many hours since I had thought of her. What was her plight now? It was growing colder and colder.

I hardly knew her. I'd seen her, yes, but that was in moonlight, and clouds darkened the earth. What colour was her hair? Fair or dark? Funny, I didn't know.

I was very cold. Everything was floating away from me.

I saw the court-room again. My other memory—how she nodded to me before she told the truth. I felt that I was there on her account.

N had listened to my thoughts.

"She nodded to you?"

"Yes."

And her eyes were before me again.

"But her eyes aren't like that," said N. "She has little, shrewd, shifty eyes that are everywhere at once. Thief's eyes."

"Thief's eyes?"

"Yes."

Suddenly N became an awful figure.

"The eyes that you saw were not hers. They were another's."

42. THE DOE

IN THE DEPTHS OF THE NIGHT, I HEARD THE doorbell ring. Could it be anyone at that hour, or had my senses played me a trick? But there it was again. I sprang out of bed, put on my dressing-gown, and left my room, to run into my landlady who stood sleepy and bewildered on the landing. She looked at me anxiously.

"Who can it be?"

I went to the door and raised my voice.

"Who's there?"

"The police."

"Heaven help us!" cried the landlady, terrified. "What have you done?"

"I?—nothing!"

Two policemen entered. They asked for the teacher. I told them I was the man they wanted.

"We've only come for information. Get into some clothes and hurry. You're coming with us—"

"Where?"

"All details later."

I dressed in bewilderment, and in a few minutes found myself in a car, with the policemen silent at my side.

Where was our destination? The smart houses came to an end, the poor quarter followed—but those ugly streets passed and we came to the villas of the rich.

"In God's name—what's happened?" I asked, in growing fear.

"We'll tell you later."

We drove on past the tramway terminus.

Now I knew.

The high gates stood open, we drove through without a pause.

The hall was full of people—among them I recognized the old porter and the footman who had shown me into the rose and gold drawing-room. A high official of the police was sitting at a table, with a clerk taking notes at his side. I was greeted by hostile looks. What was my crime, then? The official called me to him. What did he want with me?

"We have a few questions to ask you. Yesterday afternoon you wished to see this lady—" He glanced to his right.

I saw a woman in a wonderful evening frock, a woman of elegant and sheltered life—T's mother. Why was that hatred in her eyes as she stared at me?

"Answer," ordered the official.

"Yes—I wanted to speak to her, but unfortunately she had no time."

"And what did you want to tell her?"

That would have sounded absurd. I stopped. Yet I was determined to tell no lies now, for I saw the net.

"I wanted to tell this lady," I began slowly, "that I had certain definite suspicions regarding her son—"

The mother sprang up before I could get any further.

"Lies!" she shrieked. "A tissue of lies. He's guilty—he alone! *He* drove my son to his death!"

To his death? I reeled.

"What's happened, then?" I cried.

"Quiet!" ordered the official.

And now I realized that the fish had swum into the net. He lay stretched out on the land now, floundering no longer. It was finished.

An hour before, on her return home, his mother had found a note on her dressing-table: "The teacher has driven me to death." She ran to T's room, to find it empty. She spread the alarm through the house. A close search revealed nothing, whereupon the household scoured the grounds, shouting the boy's name. There was no answer.

He was found at last—near a ditch. Hanged.

His mother looked at me now. She wasn't crying. Perhaps she couldn't cry. The official showed me the note—a torn slip of paper, without signature. Suddenly I wondered: had he written something more? I looked at his mother.

"Is that all he wrote?" I asked the official.

The mother averted her eyes.

"Yes, that's all," answered the official. "Explain it."

T's mother was a beauty. I noticed that her *décolleté* was lower at the back than in front. She had certainly never known what it meant to starve. Her shoes were modish, her stockings so sheer that she appeared to wear none; but her legs were thick. Her tiny handkerchief was scented with some very expensive perfume. I couldn't recall the name of it.

But if her husband had no business, she would only have the scent of her own sweat.

Her stare was almost contemptuous now. Two bright, round eyes. What had T told me over that ice-cream?— "But I haven't got fish eyes. I've got eyes like a doe, my mother always says so." Did she say that she had too? I couldn't remember now. I looked at her. Wait, my gentle doe! Snow will fall soon, you'll run nearer to men. But I'll drive you back into the forest, where the snow lies fathom deep. You'll stay and hunger there, in ice and frost. Look at me once again, I'll speak.

43. THE OTHER EYE

AND I TOLD THEM ABOUT THE BOY WHO HAD murdered N: I told them how T always wanted to watch and to observe how a human being came into the world, and how he died. Birth and death and all that lay between—he must know everything. He would have probed into every secret, but only to remain aloof, with his own contempt. He knew no awe: it was only cowardice which composed his fear. His love for reality was but a hatred for the truth.

And as I spoke I felt, suddenly, a wonderful sense of relief that T existed no more. I was glad, glad! For in spite of one's own guilt towards him, it is splendid and beautiful when an evil-doer is destroyed.

I kept nothing back.

"There is a saw-mill that lies idle," I told them, "and there are children who sit in the windows painting dolls—"

"What has that to do with the case?"

The mother glanced out of the window, where the night lay. She appeared to be listening—for what? A step? The high gates were still open.

Suddenly I heard myself saying:

"It was absurd to try and frustrate those plans—"

T's mother stared at me again.

"It is possible that I drove your son to his death—"

I stopped.

Why was she smiling—still? Had madness come? She began to laugh—louder and louder. Hysteria: she shrieked and whimpered.

I heard only the word "God."

Then she screamed:

"It's no good!"

The others tried to calm her, but she fought them off, though the footman retained a firm hold.

"It's sawing, it's sawing!" she wailed.

What?—the saw-mill? Could she see the children in the windows? And that One who did not care whether she had time or not? For He goes through every street, great or small.

She was still fighting the others off: and she let fall a scrap of paper—as if it had been struck out of her hand. The official picked it up.

The torn, crumpled half sheet belonged to the note which had been left on the dressing-table—"The teacher has driven me to my death."

And here T had written his reason: "For he knows that I murdered N. With the stone."

An intense stillness held the room.

The mother seemed to have collapsed. She sat quite motionless now.

Suddenly she smiled again and nodded to me.

But it was not she who smiled.

Nor were those her eyes.

Still as the dark pools in the little woods of my homeland.

And sad, like children without light.

So God looked upon us here.

Once I had thought that His eyes would be malicious, piercing—but no. For God is Truth.

"Tell them it was you who broke open the box"—I heard the voice again. "Do my will and grieve me no more."

The mother went slowly up to the table and began to speak—quietly, but firmly now.

"I had wanted to spare myself the humiliation," she said. "But when the teacher mentioned the children in the windows, I thought, 'It's no good!'"

44. OVER THE SEA

TO-MORROW I AM GOING TO AFRICA.

There are flowers on my table—a parting present from my good landlady.

My parents have written to me. They are glad I have a job again, but sad because it is overseas and so far away.

There is another letter on the table too. In a blue envelope.

"Our best wishes to the negroes. —The Club."

Yesterday I went to see Eve.

She's glad the fish has been caught. The priest has promised me to take care of her when she comes out of prison.

Yes, her eyes are thief's eyes.

The prosecution has dropped the case against me, and Z is free already. I'm packing my trunk. Julius Caesar has made me a present of his death's head—so that I shan't forget him.

I must pack everything. I mustn't leave anything behind.

The nigger is going to the niggers.

THE NEVERSINK LIBRARY

THE NEVERSINK LIBRARY